HER WAN EMBRACE

Her Wan Embrace

David Barker

WEIRD HOUSE

Trade Paperback Edition

Text © 2022 by David Barker
Cover and interior art © 2022 by Dan Sauer

Editor & Publisher, Joe Morey

Copy editing and book design by F. J. Bergmann
David Barker photo by Judy Barker

ISBN: 978-1-957121-08-6

Weird House Press
Central Point, OR 97502
www.weirdhousepress.com
Join the Weird House mailing list at our website!

Dedication

For Judy

— D. B.

List of Illustrations

Table of Contents

Part 4 ~ Witches at Sunset

Part 5 ~ Victorian Tales

Part 6 ~ Hawaiian Horrors

PART 1

LIMACE OF PARIS

SMELLS OF THE NEST

Le Marais, Paris, 1894

Malora and I enjoyed an exceedingly brief—some called it hurried—courtship, having married only three months after we became acquainted. Although I gave it little thought at the time, our relationship was conducted exclusively within the constraints of an unusually limited domain; we met, discovered a mutual affection, became engaged, were wedded, and thereafter lived together entirely within the fashionable walls of La Maison de la Limace—a suite of spacious rooms on two upstairs floors of Paris' historic Place des Vosges, a luxurious seventeenth-century planned residential square (the first of its kind in the city) ideally situated in the Marais, on the Right Bank of the Seine.

It's not surprising that I was instantly taken with the beautiful and refined Malora. She had all the poise, grace, and composure of a queen, combined with the delicate sensuality of a high-bred courtesan. Without doubt, her most striking feature was her lustrous, raven-black hair, which was so long that it reached to her calves when she combed it out at night. Refusing to adapt to the constantly changing styles of Parisian fashion, when in public she always appeared attired in one of her many black silk brocade dresses, all of which modestly covered her from neck to ankle, and yet were so well-tailored to her figure that little was left to the imagination

3

concerning the perfection of her feminine charms. The austere intellectuality of her ivory forehead, the fierce independence of her piercing blue eyes, and the voluptuous promise of her pouting lips, all completed a picture of womanly perfection.

Given the striking image Malora presented, many of her male admirers (and they were legion) overestimated her height; she stood at a mere five foot in her stocking feet. Being six-foot-two inches myself, I towered over her, and yet I never noticed the discrepancy when we embraced. Whether that was due to some lucky happenstance or was proof of her crafty ways, I never really knew. All I knew is that we seemed made for one another; ours was a match forged in Heaven. Or so I believed in those ethereal first days.

Malora and her reclusive sister Camille had inherited the large and well-appointed house at Place des Vosges from their parents, along with the extensive wealth necessary to live there comfortably for the rest of their lives. Given the abundant financial resources of my new wife, I had no real need to work, but being a proud man and one who is by nature unsuited to idleness, I conducted my business affairs as if my wife were a pauper instead of a wealthy woman, and I, her only means of support. As a result of my industrious nature, along with a measure of good luck, at the time of our nuptials I was earning an income that more than met the material needs of the entire household, consisting of not only ourselves but also Malora's shiftless uncle, a delinquent nephew, two frivolous nieces, and her indolent sister. Beyond that, I supported the sizable staff needed to properly run such a household, and did so cheerfully, never once begrudging any expense that I was called upon to satisfy.

The magnificence and beauty of our home could hardly be overstated. The Place des Vosges had enjoyed a long and colorful history. Before acquiring its present name in 1800, it was known as Place Royale, a square surrounded by thirty-six identical houses constructed under orders from King Henri IV. The structure was completed in 1612 on the site of the old Hôtel des Tournelles, which itself dated back to the fourteenth century and had been owned by a succession of French kings.

The square's history is peppered with macabre incidents, any one of which when taken alone is not cause for undue alarm. But when these curiosities are considered together, they suggest that an unwholesome influence may have been at work within the walls of Hôtel des Tournelles, and after it, Place des Vosges. The lavishly bizarre "Dance of Death" was celebrated there in 1451, along with other festivities of a disturbing nature. In 1524, the German magician and occultist, Agrippa de Nettesheim, resided within Hôtel des Tournelles. A reputed necromancer, he is alleged to have made the dead appear before the duchess Louise de Savoie. King Henri II died of agonizing wounds sustained at the old Hôtel during a jousting tournament in 1559, after which the derelict building was demolished by his widow, Catherine de Medici, in 1563. Later, the deserted site was used as a horse market and a gunpowder magazine. Since its inauguration as a planned square, many illustrious persons have lived at Place des Vosges, including the novelist Victor Hugo (himself an occultist), who occupied rooms in what at the time was known as Hôtel de Rohan Guémenée.

The darker aspects of the square's past were belied by the charm of its two-story townhouses faced with white stone and red brick, a street-level arcade of vaulted arches, and steep roofs featuring dormer windows and blue slate tiles. Within the square, protected from the harsh realities of the city, lay a peaceful, tree-lined garden where lovers strolled, and children played. Fountains stood at the four corners of the broad lawn, while the center held an 1829 bronze statue of Louis XIII on horseback.

Our union soon proved to be fruitful; we had just entered the sere summer season when Malora informed me that we would be blessed with a child. At that time, she advised me that it was customary in her family that when one of the women became pregnant, the lady would withdraw from the outer world and go into seclusion for the duration of gestation, hiding herself away within the recesses of the home, and henceforth shunning social interaction with all but the maids who attended her. Malora's uncle, nephew, nieces, and sister retired from public life at the same time, and henceforth I only saw them on the rare occasions when they came and went on unavoidable errands. On that fateful day, all teas, dinners, and other occasions for socializing at Maison de la Limace suddenly ceased, and outside visitors were no longer admitted, under instructions from Malora. If I needed to meet with a business associate, I would arrange to join them at some nearby location outside the confines of the Maison.

This overnight cessation of social events was a radical change in the mood that had prevailed within the home. I went from living what had often amounted to a public existence within the Maison to at times feeling somewhat isolated as I walked about the empty rooms. Whereas previously I had grown accustomed to sharing each day with Malora, now I seldom saw her, or anyone else for that matter, other than an occasional chance encounter with one of the servants. A more attentive husband might have lamented the sudden loss of his wife's company in this manner, but I was so busy with my business concerns that I only passively noticed her absence. On any given day she might spend at most five minutes with me, either in the morning while I had breakfast, or during my afternoon tea. Whole days would often pass without my seeing her at all, although she would seldom fail to have a note carried to me advising me of her condition and inquiring after my own well-being.

I saw this separation between us as a perhaps necessary but unfortunate inconvenience and one that was surely temporary in nature. What I did not realize is that it would become the norm in our relationship, for she—and the rest of her family—remained in seclusion after our first daughter was born in March 1895, being reclusive almost all the time, day and night. Once she had recovered from the medical effects of childbirth, she did sometimes slip into my chamber late at night and give herself to me as of old, but she never stayed for very long, and I became used to waking alone in our bed during the quiet hours after midnight.

Around that time, I began to strongly suspect that Malora and our infant child—as well as my in-laws—had begun to inhabit the lower levels under the Maison, but I had no specific knowledge of exactly where they might be. Late one night, unable to sleep, I impulsively arose from bed, pulled on a dressing gown, and descended the back stairway into the gloomy subterranean portion of the dwelling. I don't know what I expected to see down there: perhaps Malora rocking the baby to sleep in a corner of the cellar that had been made comfortable with a bed, a crib, and the myriad items needed for tending to a newborn. But that is not what happened. I saw Malora, all right, but she was alone. The baby was not with her.

As I ambled slowly down a dank corridor, idly peering right and left into the primitive chambers arrayed on either side, a darkly attired feminine figure moving quickly down an intersecting corridor abruptly crossed my path, startling me. She was in my view for only a second, and I don't believe she saw me. I had no chance to study her, so briefly was she in my sight, and yet I had the distinct impression that something was dreadfully wrong with her. It was nothing I could put my finger on. She did not appear to be ill—indeed, my impression was quite the opposite; her entire being seemed to be animated by some strangely intense transcendent energy, as if she enjoyed too much of the life force. Beyond that, I had the distinct idea that I was not supposed to see her in her current condition—whatever that may have been.

That for me to observe her thusly was forbidden. But forbidden by whom? And for what reason?

Myriad questions came to mind. Where was she going in such a hurry? Had someone summoned her at that late hour? For what imaginable purpose? Who in the household possibly could have held that much authority over Malora, the mistress of the Maison? I could think of no satisfying answers. This bizarre nocturnal encounter left me deeply unsettled for days. I tried to banish it from memory, and never mentioned it to Malora.

A year later in March 1896, a second daughter was born, followed by a son in December 1898 and then a third daughter in March 1901, all within the span of only six years. Malora's cloistered lifestyle remained unchanged throughout the period in which our family was formed, and it continued after our final child entered this world. I accepted it as a given: this was how she chose to live her life—near me but seldom actually beside me.

Malora's abstinence from any form of social life early in our marriage came as something of a surprise to me, because before her first pregnancy the house had been a veritable hub of social activity characterized by a steady stream of visitors, as well as being the site of countless parties, dances and other manner of festive celebrations occurring at least weekly if not on a more frequent basis. Malora had clearly enjoyed these social events, and she did much of the planning for them. It was at just such a gathering in the apartment's opulent ballroom that we had first met—a function to which I had been invited due to my involvement in a rather dreary business arrangement with one of her cousins, a pleasant but dull-witted young woman named Juliette. How vividly I recall being introduced to Malora by this cousin. As the latter and I exchanged inane pleasantries, I studied the rococo panels lining the ballroom's ceiling, their gilded frames glowing in the light of the chandeliers. Then my gaze fell to the red velvet curtains that cloaked the tall windows, before fixing itself upon a small coterie comprised of four elegant young ladies that stood with masterful composure before one of the windows. Three of these ladies wore white satin gowns; Malora alone was garbed in rich, lustrous black. The contrast in attire, along with her remarkable grace and beauty, made Malora the natural center of attention within the group, and the obvious envy of all the other ladies in attendance that evening. I did not know her name at that moment but immediately made it my business to learn it, along with everything else that I might discover about this mysterious woman.

Now, in sad contrast to those happy former times, the house was always still and devoid of merriment, for even when the children were present, they were studiously quiet, occupied as they constantly were with their drawing, reading, handicrafts, and other meditative activities. My visits with them almost never included Malora. Rather, their nanny would usher them in, oversee their behavior, and then lead them away again when she judged they had spent enough time in my presence. Whether or not Malora enjoyed some sort of privileged access to the nursery or spent time with the children elsewhere was unknown to me. I assumed that she had final say in all matters relating to the children and their upbringing, and that seemed proper to me.

Many were the times when I asked Malora where exactly in the house I might find her own bedchamber, as well as the nursery in which our children played, ate, were educated, and slept, if in fact the nursery were a room separate from her own. They clearly did not spend any time on the upstairs floors where I passed countless hours alone. Presumable, they, Malora, and the rest of her family were elsewhere in the structure—below.

There certainly was sufficient space for the children upstairs, but that was a resource Malora chose not to use. We had a comfortable parlor; a lovely, though somewhat dark, drawing room, whimsically furnished with eccentric cabinets, tables and mirrors that her father had gathered during his travels around the globe; a warm, if small, kitchen, the ceiling of which was lined with bright copper tiles; two small bed chambers—also quite dark—that had formerly been occupied by Malora and myself, but one of which now stood glaringly empty; two larger bed chambers formerly shared by her uncle and nephew in one case, and her sister and nieces in the other; the above-mentioned spacious ballroom; a long and narrow dining room whose many windows overlooked the square's central garden; an irregularly shaped room the size of a walk-in closet that was crowded with overstuffed bookcases and an imposing oak desk (my so-called "study"); and a modest-sized water closet with black and white checkered floor tiles, white porcelain sink and tub, and polished brass spigots. None of these rooms held a single cradle or diminutive bed. No articles of children's clothing were to be found in any of the dressers, cabinets, or trunks furnishing these rooms. Repeatedly, I asked Malora where she and the children stayed. She would never give me a direct answer. Rather, she would make vague pronouncements that I suspected were intended as much to discourage such inquiries as to answer them.

An example is that late one afternoon as we watched the rose-hued orb of the sun sinking below the dusky horizon from the third-floor balcony, she declared: "What I love about this house is that it's not just these three floors in a charming old building. It's much more than that. There are older structures below, rude stone constructions that predate this relatively modern dwelling. Many floors of them, in fact, extending deep into the earth. Basements, subterranean levels, crypts, tunnels, sewers, catacombs—they extend out in all directions, endlessly. The house communicates with the entire city, just as the present communicates with the past and the future, seamlessly, without break or interruption. I love that infinitude, the eternal quality of this house and its connecting structures. It has no limit, no beginning nor end. Much like our love, my dear. It goes out in all directions, and in the end, it all leads back to here."

Those were the last words she uttered to me that day. They were still impressing themselves upon my mind when she abruptly arose, gave me what I took to be a rather stern look—as if to warn me not to follow her back down to where she was retreating—and then, oddly, backed away from me in a most peculiar manner, as one who is walking backward, unnaturally, while continuing to look straight ahead. At that instant I had the strangest impression that something was physically drawing her away from me—some long tendril or uncanny limb that formed an integral part of her biology, something that was cleverly concealed behind her back, being hidden by the fullness of her dark feminine attire with its many silken skirts and ruffled petticoats and taking advantage of its perspective relative to me in a way that rendered this connecting appendage literally invisible to me, although I did somehow sense its malign presence.

I slept poorly that night, tossing and turning in my bed with its tall posts of dark walnut towering around me, and beyond them, the overpowering red-damask-lined walls, which constantly pressed in upon me as I wrestled with my demons. I had always sensed something disturbing in this gloomy, ill-lit chamber, but while Malora had shared it with me, I was able to suppress those negative feelings. Now, with her total absence after sunset each day, the room's adverse effect on me was unabated. For hours I was molested by feverish nightmares of a maze of buried passageways that grew downward, streaming out of our house and outward across the city's substructure like the myriad roots of a long-established tree. In this horrid dream I gained the unwelcome knowledge that Malora, my beloved wife and the mother of my children, was integrally connected to and one with this hellish network of living tissue—that the infernal entity had become an undifferentiated part of her being and that she was but

11

one of many organs in its vast, diffuse body. Roaming unwisely through the ancient subterranean shafts below the city—be they of Roman, Gallic, medieval, or Renaissance origin—I caught an unforgettable glimpse of this malignant creature as a broad section of its extensive organism slithered past me, coating the time-worn stone walls of the tunnel with thick, gray, viscous slime.

Although morning eventually came and filled the house with soothing light and warmth, I was unable to dispel the pervasive sense of gloom that had accompanied this terrible dream and found that staying in the residence alone throughout the day when I wasn't out on business matters proved too oppressive to my spirit. Thus, I resolved that I would change my habits, and from that day forward, I passed all my free time at a small bamboo table positioned under a red-and-white-tiled arch in one of the cafés occupying the long arcade that circled the building on the ground floor. From there I would gaze out at the freshly mown lawns of the square's courtyard, sipping coffee and studying the passersby as they crossed before the nearby two-tiered stone fountain on their unknowable errands along the walkway. In time, my friends and associates came to understand that they could find me there at any given hour and would come by to talk or just sit and drink silently in my company. The business associates tended to ignore my moodiness, but my friends had an intuitive understanding that I was suffering under the weight of oppressive circumstances in my personal life. Sometimes they would gently inquire after Malora. "How is she doing?" they would ask. "We never see her anymore."

"Nor do I," I would answer, sipping at my coffee and looking away, not wanting to meet their gaze. "Nor do I."

"And the children?"

"I see very little of them these days, either. They are so busy with their studies, and all of their needs are met by the servants and nannies."

"Well, your family may be too busy for you of late, but your friends are always there."

"I appreciate that." And then they would stand up, visibly embarrassed by my melancholia, and leave me in peace.

I usually brought a book with me, and when I didn't have company I would read, although in the late afternoons I would often lay the book aside and pass the remaining minutes before sunset watching the portions of sky that were visible from my table, always enchanted by the rich hues the light took on as it deepened in shade from a pale rose to a vivid scarlet. This daily ritual always called to mind the comforting fact that I was outside, above the ground, free of whatever evil thing might lie below the cobblestones of the roads and the slate slabs lining basement floors, for I could never erase from memory the entity I sensed had become stealthily attached to Malora and that I feared she had become permanently bonded to within the occult recesses of the city's archaic structures.

One afternoon in May 1902, when I had just placed a tattered volume of Gothic tales face down on the table and taken a sip of hot coffee, our maintenance man approached from out of the crowd and asked if he might have a word with me. A stout, barrel-chested fellow with a drooping moustache and balding pate, he was a humble laborer who clearly felt out of place at an elegant Place des Vosges café.

"Certainly, Gregor. How may I help you?"

"Sir, I don't mean to disturb you, but something has come up which I feel I should discuss with you, as master of the house."

He looked quite nervous and seemed agitated, as if he feared being caught consulting with me.

"What is it? You can speak freely."

"The lady of the house, Madame Malora, has instructed me to make a modification to the building, and I feel I should have your opinion before I proceed with making this change."

"Well, as you surely know, Malora and her sister are the sole owners of the Maison, and they have complete authority when it comes to running the house. You must follow their orders to the letter and do whatever they ask of you. You don't need my permission to carry out their instructions. I'm sure whatever it is they have asked of you, they have considered it well and made a wise decision on a course of action."

"But still, sir, with all due respect, they are refined ladies and do not have the same understanding that a man with callouses on his hands has when it comes to matters of the repair and upkeep of buildings. Although of course I will do as they ask, I would like to have your opinion on the work to be done and whatever advice you care to share for the successful completion of the task before I carry out the order."

"That's an old-fashioned way to look at things, Gregor, and some would argue that it unfairly discounts the abilities of the fairer sex, but I see no harm in giving you whatever thoughts I may have on the matter. What is it they have asked you to do?"

"The lady wants me to knock a hole in a wall, in an old passageway several stories below ground level."

"A small hole for running plumbing or wiring through?"

"No, sir, a large hole. Four, maybe five feet across."

"Indeed, that's a big hole. Whatever for?"

"She says that it is needed—by someone or something she declines to name—*to provide egress*. Those were her exact words, sir: 'to provide egress.'"

I told him to do as she requested. I said that those old structures down there are strong and can generally withstand such changes, but do it carefully so as not to risk a collapse of the wall, which could be supporting other parts of the building.

He said he would do so, but he would still feel better if I came along with him first and took a look at what he was talking about. And so, we left my table in the arcade, left the warm afternoon sun which felt so comforting on our shoulders, and entered through a huge, old, battered wooden door, pocked with iron bolts, that was set into a sturdy archway on the side of the building. Immediately beyond this door, the floor gave way to a steep stairway of rough-hewn stone that we took down to the lower levels of the house, and below those, even deeper into the primitive structures over which the house had been constructed some three hundred years before.

"This area has great age," said Gregor as he brushed cobwebs from our path along a crudely paved corridor. "It is many hundreds of years old."

"The main house was built in the early 1600s," I informed him, "But these basement levels date back to the thirteenth century. I've never had a chance to examine them in any detail, as Malora considers the lower levels to be her exclusive domain— one that I'm not encouraged to explore."

"Nor am I, sir. The lady is very particular about who may enter this area and how far they may go within it. I keep to those spaces in which she has given me permission to work. Everything else is off-limits."

Realizing that Gregor had visited a much larger portion of the lower levels than I had, I took the opportunity to ask him about the nursery.

"Have you ever seen it?"

"No, sir, I have not."

"But do you know where it is?"

He turned and gave me a pained expression, as if he were struggling with his conscience. "I can say this much, sir. While I have not been told by the lady precisely where the nursery is located, I could guess as much, based on an odor I have detected on occasion in the more remote, archaic spaces below the house."

"What sort of odor?"

15

"In many of the derelict chambers and connecting passageways I have noticed the musty scent of old stone dust and the dampness of the ages, and that is a common smell down here. However, a few times as I approached a certain extremely old and dilapidated area, I noticed a much different aroma. I don't know what it is called, but it is a powerful stench—one that the other servants and I refer to as 'smells of the nest.' It is rich and pungent, and not at all pleasant in the nostrils."

"Smells of the nest," I repeated. I thought about that for a moment. "A nursery is a kind of nest, isn't it? And you believe this odor signals the proximity of the nursery?"

"I do, sir."

"Tell me more about this odor, Gregor."

"It is like the sulfurous stink of rotten eggs, sir. The foul air of fecundity. When it fills your nose, it causes you to have dark thoughts of unnatural creatures being conceived and born. Thoughts of when a woman's water breaks, and the infant emerges, screaming and gasping for air. It is the smell of violence and the relentless force of life making itself known to the world."

"It sounds quite nasty."

"It is, sir."

At the end of the corridor was a stairway leading down into utter darkness. The steepness of the steps and variations in the size of blocks used in the stairway's construction suggested that it was from Roman times. Some of the blocks were cracked, some had crumbling edges, and the areas where men had trod were worn smooth from centuries of use. Gregor led the way with his lantern.

"We are almost there," he said with a grateful tone.

It was a short distance to the wall in question. Soon Gregor was standing before it, pointing first to a stone on the left, then to another on the right. "All this material between the two stones comes out," he said, indicating the width of the hole he was about

16

to make. I didn't see any structural problems with the plan. A pair of primitive Doric columns provided support to the ceiling on either side of the proposed hole. It didn't look like that part of the wall was doing much work toward holding things in place. Even if it were, the blocks there were large and appeared to be thick; whatever material remained after Gregor made the hole should be adequate.

"I think if you keep the hole only that wide and no more, and proceed with caution, you should be successful. Just to be safe, you might want to erect a couple of timbers on either side to help bolster the ceiling."

"That is a good suggestion, sir."

"What's behind there? Solid earth, or open space?"

"I don't know, sir. This morning when I was looking at the wall and thinking how I might do the work, where I would strike the first blow of the hammer, I thought I heard something."

"Something on the other side?"

"Perhaps. It was hard to tell where it was coming from. There was a low, rumbling vibration, the floor shook a little, and I thought I heard a muffled sound of something brushing past quickly, a sound like wet skin rubbing against polished marble. I thought it came from the other side of the wall, through the cracks between the blocks, but I was unsure."

What he described sounded like the damnable thing I had witnessed in my terror-filled dream: an expanse of gray flesh as huge as the side of an ox, sliding through a long and twisting subterranean channel, contracting and expanding, the undulating locomotion of some serpentine devil in flight. It called to mind the hidden tendril that had dragged Malora away from me that afternoon when I first sensed that something was dreadfully wrong in our home.

"Well, whatever is behind there, you'll find out soon enough. Do as the lady asks, and be careful, Gregor."

17

I left him down there contemplating the rough expanse of ancient wall, immediately went up to my gloomy bedroom on the third floor of the house, and packed a bag with some clothes, a few important papers, and enough cash to see me through for a while. Then I wrote a carefully worded note to Malora, regretfully explaining my decision to remove myself from the house, and left it on her favorite Chinese dresser, to find on her next visit upstairs.

My new residence was in a small hotel on the *rue* Mouffetard in the Latin Quarter. Before I would take the room, I insisted to the landlord that I must see the basement. I'm sure he thought me an eccentric but nonetheless allowed me to examine every nook and cranny of the ancient cellar for the presence of exterior doors, stairwells, false walls, connecting passageways, and any other means of ingress and egress. All I found, thankfully, was a coal bin and a rack of dusty wine bottles. He generously offered me one of the bottles, a Pinot Noir of fine vintage, and I accepted, although I knew that one bottle alone would not be sufficient when, later that afternoon, I would sit out on the balcony, gazing at a prospect of the city and attempting to fully eradicate from mind the blasphemies I believed occurred in the uncharted crypts and nighted wells of horror that lay below La Maison de la Limace.

THOSE

Those dismissed as superstition
carry out a somber mission.
Just beyond life's fringe they dwell,
reaching out from deepest Hell.
Probing into lives benign,
twisting them in ways malign.

Entities defying reason
thrive in this decaying season.
Sensing the approach of Death,
they inhale each mournful breath.
Guard against these or regret
the slew of woe you thus beget.

Here beside us they reside;
by no laws do they abide.
There's a kingdom they have wrought
just beyond the edge of thought.
Ignore these specters at your peril;
from their core flows hatred feral.

Her Wan Embrace

Latin Quarter, Paris, 1902

I had foolishly believed that my hotel in the Latin Quarter was far enough away from the Marais as to be beyond the grasp of the pernicious entity that had subtly invaded our home in La Maison de la Limace, secretly seized control of my wife, Malora, and, ultimately forced me to flee the family nest one dreadful May day in a desperate bid to preserve my very existence as an independent human being, not to mention my sanity. But, alas, it was not far enough by a long shot, as I soon learned. The entity held the advantage of dominating a wide network of subterranean tunnels and passageways throughout central Paris and enjoyed full access to almost every structure in the Latin Quarter, as well as most of the buildings in the other *arrondissements* clustered around either bank of the Seine.

My first two months in the Quarter were spent in blissful ignorance of the danger I continued to live under, as I daily strolled the cobblestone lined paths of the *rue* Mouffetard, curious as to what new experiences my sudden status as a solitary man might lead. I was not compelled to labor at any mundane occupation, having accumulated considerable wealth during the busy years in which our family was established, and thus could easily provide for the material needs of myself, my wife, our three daughters, one son, and Malora's extended family, without any risk of exhausting the majority of my funds. Simply put, I was a man of means, free to use my time as I saw fit. Having long been intrigued by the visual arts, I began to toy with the idea that I might become a painter myself, and soon developed the habit of dropping in on galleries throughout the Quarter to see the new work being done by my fellow Left Bank artists. I also formed a habit of entering every church, chapel and cathedral I encountered on my walks, as I took deep solace in studying the religious imagery adorning these ancient sanctuaries.

One afternoon in August, before I had become fully aware of the continuing danger all about me, I ducked into a fifteenth-century church in the fifth *arrondissement.* A mass had just concluded, and a noisy throng of worshipers brushed past me, impatiently making their exit from the church as I proceeded, somewhat timidly, in the opposite direction, toward the now-abandoned altar. Passing a dark alcove to my left, I heard a soft but distinct sighing sound, as if some frail creature of the shadows were trying to catch my attention in spite of the boisterous competition being provided by the talkative parishioners. Halting, I turned and stared into the gloomy recess but could discern no figure there, no lurker who might be the source of this strange mewling which I could not decide was more a breathless, sickly gasping or the random soughing of a stray wind through the cavernous hollows of the stony structure.

"Hither ... Come hither...." it seemed to say. I took a few steps toward the dim alcove and listened again. Then it uttered:

"Prithee ... Prithee...."

"Prithee?" I asked. One of the departing devout stared at me as if I were mad, but I ignored her impudence and queried the shadows once more. "Did you say 'Prithee,' unseen one?"

"Yea, Prithee. Indeed, I pray thee, sir, please step in. Away from the crowd. They should not hear what I shall tell."

Each word from this unseen personage was more an airy whisper than a fully uttered statement, and yet, I clearly understood her intent—for the owner of the voice was decidedly feminine, so tender and delicate were her tones.

Fearing I might be acting unwisely by heeding an unseen voice, I nonetheless stepped away from the stream of parishioners flowing toward the church doors and entered the dark alcove. My eyes adjusted and shortly thereafter I was able to make out an imposing marble statue of a female saint whom I did not recognize occupying the center of the alcove. Behind her the wall was lined with ornately carved wooden panels decorated with richly hued paintings and thick gold leaf. Narrow spaces between the foremost panels provided a limited view of other panels set in the dark recesses beyond.

My attention was drawn to a spot behind the statue—a particularly shadowy area between two front panels that was about a foot wide. As I watched this area with mounting expectancy, a long and slender hand slowly emerged from behind the gilded wood, wrapping its unnaturally thin fingers around the panel's edge. A pale, elongated face followed it, then the hint of a robe-garbed shoulder as the thing leaned far enough into the opening to establish eye contact with me. When it did so, the creature's entire being lit up, her eyes flaring with an inner blaze. I fear I blushed at the profound intimacy of this moment, for I felt as if this ethereal being had the power to virtually peer into my soul and read there the sorrows that had plagued me since the unfortunate day when I discovered an unholy malignancy had infested my home and taken captive my cherished family, holding them in slavish thrall to its unknown desires.

I should explain that I was deeply puzzled by this being's remarkable appearance, for it was simultaneously unutterably beautiful, in an unearthly way, and shockingly terrible, bearing all the signs of advanced physical corruption, such as one might

23

see in a newly unearthed corpse that has lain below the ground for centuries. That it lived and breathed there could be no doubt, but was the life force it exhibited a solely material energy in sympathy with the natural order of things, or was it driven by something fantastical and paranormal? I did not know and dared not ask.

"Do not fear me. I am not the foe of any man," she whispered airily.

"I'm not afraid of you, or not too much, anyway. But I do have my apprehensions. The world is not what I once thought it to be."

"There are things in this world that a wise man rightly ought to fear, but I am not one of those. Do you trust me?"

"I suppose I do."

"Trust and an open heart are commendable qualities, when accompanied by reasoned caution. You were prudent to leave the home you shared with Malora. In its depths a woman of her kind may thrive, as may her offspring, but you were in peril."

"I sensed that, and although it broke my heart, I had to flee."

"But you are still in great peril in this district, far from the Marais. That which you thought you had escaped followed you here. It tracks your every movement, slithers within walls as you cower in your bed. There can be no safety for you in the Latin Quarter. You must remove yourself further ... much further away."

The ethereal being's voice trailed off. She pulled back, and I could no longer see her head, and then only her slender fingers remained in sight, grasping the edge of the carved wood, until they, too, slipped away, one by one.

*

Hurrying back toward my room, I had the impression that the once carefree *rue* Mouffetard now seethed with sinister unwholesomeness. Everywhere I saw the traces of ancient structures that

24

I knew underlay the modern buildings. Below the street level, all the buildings of Paris were connected by an endless maze of subterranean tunnels, subbasements, catacombs, crypts, and natural caves that had been hideously augmented by reckless excavation. Not a single structure seemed to remain untouched by the myriad of interconnecting spaces below ground. And the insidious slug-like entity that slithered through dark passageways beneath La Maison de la Limace also had unlimited access to the cafes, restaurants, shops, and hotels that lined the *rue* Mouffetard. By the time I reached my hotel, I had resolved to immediately relocate to higher ground.

Often, while sitting at a table outside a nearby café, I had admired the distant silhouette of Montmartre rising above the skyline of the Right Bank, crowned by the white domed basilica of Sacré-Coeur. Home to many of Paris' renegade and bohemian artists, Montmartre had long beguiled me. Perched as it was hundreds of feet above the surrounding city, I assumed it lay beyond the reach of the degenerate entity that plagued the heart of Paris. Reaching my room, I hastily scrawled a note of apology to my landlord which I left on the table, threw a few things into a battered suitcase, and departed. In ten minutes, I was on a Metro train leaving the Latin Quarter, headed for Montmartre. A short while after that, I walked the hilly streets of that storied district, in search of a room. To my frenzied mind, the golden afternoon light acted as a calming balm—the air clear and cool—and for the first time in months I felt free and at peace, although true happiness was of course impossible, given my forced isolation from wife and family.

That afternoon I found a suitable room set on a high hillside above a small vineyard. My window, which I formed the habit of keeping open day and night to allow the wind to flow unimpeded, gave a clear view of the Paris that I once had loved but now feared to the point of abhorrence. In this room, tucked away above the

25

hilltop village, I found enough mental tranquility to paint during the sun-washed mornings, although sleeping through the long nocturnal hours proved impossible, given the hellish nightmares that plagued me with their grotesque visions of burrowing, contracting, and expanding gastropodous monstrosities. It was only in the warm, quiet afternoons that I was able to achieve some much-needed rest, lying sprawled upon the bed beside the open window, listening to the muted distant sounds of the village until wispy dreams of my prior harmonious domestic life flooded into my sorrow-wracked brain.

On one such afternoon on the last day of September 1902, I was deep in peaceful slumber when I sensed that someone was lying beside me, prone upon the unmade bed, their shoulder gently pressed against my back. Coming awake with a start, I abruptly sat up and turned to see who it was that had so boldly intruded into my room uninvited and joined me in my bed. My sudden movements aroused my guest, and she in turn sat up and faced me. With unspeakable shock I recognized the peculiar being whom I had encountered in an alcove of the Latin Quarter church.

This mysterious feminine being, who in the murky shadows of the ancient church had exhibited a sickly pallor, now appeared positively radiant in the warm glow of the afternoon sun. As before, she was garbed in a long, flowing robe, the antique fabric of which was decayed and tattered. I had never seen anyone with such a long, thin face, nor with such slender, bony fingers. The lady's flaxen-hued hair, which reached to her shoulders, hung limply against her skull, lacking all luster. When she finally spoke, her voice was just as I remembered it from our first meeting— airy, breathless, and ethereal.

"Yea, I have followed thee, for thine own protection and well-being."

I was puzzled by this statement, for I didn't know why I

still needed her protection now that I had left behind the lower regions of the city.

"But why ..." I began to inquire, when she stopped me short by reaching out her thin, spindly hand—the skin of which resembled yellowed parchment—and gently brushed her long nails against my forehead, sending me back into a deep, dreamless slumber that lasted until the violet rays of twilight fell across the bed.

*

As nightfall devoured the substance of Montmartre in its gloomy maw, I left my apartment and walked the short distance of a few steep, twisting blocks to a well-lit cabaret that was a popular hangout for bohemian artists and their models. Due to the warning I had been given by the female being that afternoon, I knew I would be unable to sleep, so disturbed was my mind by thoughts of the malignant creatures who plagued the subterranean realms of Paris, including this peaceful village that had formerly seemed so safely positioned above the city proper. There I found a multitude of acquaintances, song and dance, and generously flowing drink, all of which helped me to forget for a few hours the peril we all faced. I was deep into my third glass of wine when I felt a large, rough hand on my shoulder and heard the deep, friendly voice of Gregor, who had been our maintenance man at La Maison de la Limace at the time I had left.

"Pardon the interruption, sir. It's just that I am startled to see you here. I've had no word of your whereabouts or situation since the day you departed La Maison."

"Gregor! It's good to see you again! Please join me in a glass."

"Oh, no, sir. I couldn't impose...."

"I insist." I pulled out a chair and tugged at his arm until he seated himself. Then I motioned to the waiter for a round of drinks for the two of us.

"What brings you here, Gregor?"

"My sister—the unmarried one. She works as a maid in a great house on the hill. I visit her once a month. I've been in this establishment many times, but this is the first I've seen you here, sir."

"I recently moved to Montmartre, to escape that horrid thing we discussed at La Maison. Prior to that, I had a room in the Latin Quarter, but it proved no safer there than in the Marais. It seems the thing is everywhere—even in Montmartre, it turns out."

"Indeed. That is my understanding as well, sir. There are a great many holy crypts in the old abandoned gypsum quarries that pockmark the hills of Montmartre, and I am told the creatures that we detected at La Maison may be found in those sacred chambers as well. Nowhere in Paris seems to be free of these monstrosities."

We sat quietly for two or three minutes, meditating on this unfortunate situation. Finally, I broke the silence. "Tell me Gregor, how fares Madame Malora? Is she still a recluse, secluded in the basement of the house, and in the deeper levels below that?"

"She is, sir, I'm sorry to report. I seldom see her anymore, but when I do, I am always greatly shocked at her condition. The creature we spoke of appears to be taking over her entire being. I have seen evidence of this with my own eyes. Although Madame has always dressed modestly, being well covered from head to foot, on the rare occasions when I have accidentally glimpsed her wrist or neck, it is quite apparent to me that the flesh there has much changed. It now has an unhealthy purplish tint to it, sir, and the sticky translucence of a mucous membrane."

"Are her movements quite peculiar and unnatural, as before?"

"More so. She seems to be merely a puppet, a fleshy polyp at the end of the creature's outstretched tendril, rather than an actual person. When she addresses me, it's like speaking with the creature, rather than with Madame. I do believe—and it grieves

28

me tremendously to say this—that the abomination has almost completely taken her over, sir, and that very little of the Madame we knew and loved is left on this earth."

I wanted to inquire about the state of the children, but was afraid of what his answer might be, and so I changed the subject to something neutral, asking about various people with whom I had conducted business while living in the Marais."

"All of those gentlemen are well and prospering, sir, except for Monsieur Le Bon. Sadly, he suffered a tragic fate."

"In what way?"

"Monsieur Le Bon was murdered shortly after you left. His eviscerated corpse was found in the basement of Musée de Cluny, in the Roman baths area known as the Frigidarium. According to the newspapers, the man's internal organs had been suctioned from the abdominal cavity in a highly bizarre manner."

"What a terrible thing. I'll send flowers to his widow with a note of condolence."

"I'm sure she would appreciate that, sir."

We had both drained our cups, and although I urged Gregor to stay for another round, he begged off, claiming he had to rise early the next morning and needed his rest.

*

Bleary-eyed with exhaustion, I dragged myself home in the early hours when all of Montmartre was hushed and the narrow alleys were plunged into impenetrable darkness. As before, I could not sleep, my brain over-excited by excess of drink as well as the ghastly news of Le Bon's death and the always-present menace of the horrific slug-like entities that had driven me first from my home, and then from the Quarter, and that now threatened to compel my departure from Montmartre. When daylight finally came, I painted for an hour, badly—the colors muddied and the forms ill-defined—and then collapsed on the disheveled bed, hoping

29

for a surcease to anxiety. Dreamless oblivion washed over me, drowning me in blissful nothingness. Hours passed, after which I slowly, gradually drifted toward consciousness. My first real sense of my surroundings—that I was sleeping in my room and it was the warm, sun-filled afternoon of October 1st—came when I felt a lithe body gently pressing against my own. A woman's body, long and curvaceous, and desperately frail. This was, I knew, the mysterious feminine being whom I had twice before encountered. Not startled this time, as I had been when I first awoke beside her in this same bed the day before, I opened my eyes, saw that it was indeed she, and sat up, fixing my questioning gaze upon her pallid features.

"Exactly who are you?" I asked, in a tone I hoped was kind.

She stared into my eyes for a moment, detected that my mood was one of curiosity rather than antagonism, and smiled subtly. "I am Azrael, whom some call the Angel of Death."

"Azrael—that's an unusual name. What does it mean?"

"It means 'the Help that Arrives.' I assist those who are worthy, and in need—such as yourself."

"How will you assist me?"

"I will teach you to banish *La Limace* from your life—the demon that has consumed your wife and in time may consume your children."

"Teach me, then."

*

I followed her to the Montmartre Cemetery, noticing that none of the people we passed paid any attention to my strange companion. It was as if she were invisible to all but me, and perhaps she was. My guide seemed to know exactly where she was going, while I soon became disoriented in following her up and down the many paths, along cobblestone streets and passing under a rusted iron bridge. In an obscure corner off the beaten path, she led me to a stone doorway that opened between two ruined mausoleums. There we descended further below street level, into the vast, uncharted caverns of an abandoned chalk quarry with its innumerable centuries-old crypts that had served as secret chapels in days gone by.

Finally, we reached our destination: one of the ancient crypts that strongly smelled of dampness and decay.

"Stand quietly beside me in this spot between the sarcophagi," whispered Azrael, "where we may observe without being observed. Do not move or speak. *La Limace* will arrive in time, unaware of our presence. Make no motion, and do not fear. No harm shall come to thee while I am about."

"I understand."

Azrael bent over and picked up the shard of a burnt-out torch that lay on the ground below a wall-mounted stanchion. Its tip had been reduced by fire to soft charcoal. She broke off a piece of this greasy black substance and used it to mark upon my forehead a bold sigil that I assumed was intended to protect me from the creature.

"This is the Mark of Help that Arrives. The foul one recognizes the power of its form and will not challenge it."

"I hope you're right about that."

She touched a long finger to her thin lips, urging me to silence, and as she did so the hunched-over figure of an elderly monk in a brown hooded robe shuffled around a distant corner and made his way toward us down a long aisle between rows of caskets lining the walls, unaware that he was not alone in the chamber. As he neared our position, he turned another corner just a few feet from us and shuffled away to our left. At that moment I saw the awful thing that had been concealed behind him during his journey down the aisle: a thick, slimy limb that ran the length of the path he had just walked and turned where he had turned, following the monk as he shambled along. The front end of this

31

monstrous limb, which was a sort of oily-skinned tentacle, came up behind the man and entered a gap in the fabric at the back of his robe, suggesting the obscene possibility that the limb had attached itself to, or was even a part of, the man's body. At the sight of this I almost issued an involuntary gasp, but the radiant eyes of my companion stopped me from making any utterance.

"Now," she whispered airily, "Step forward and show thyself to the monk."

I did so, and the effect was immediate. The man shrieked, his eyes wild with dread, while the slimy limb of the slug-like brute that was in command of his body contracted violently, pulling the monk backward so rapidly that he lost his footing, but it didn't matter, for the strong sinews of the creature's limb held him upright as the monster recoiled and drew the flailing monk back into the black recesses from which it had emerged. Simultaneously, the mucus-coated flesh of the creature shriveled and cracked while emitting vapors, suggesting a toxic reaction in the beast to the presence of the sigil, or perhaps to her who had drawn it.

Relieved by this miraculous event, I turned to heartily thank my companion, but she had suddenly departed, or preternaturally vanished, leaving me alone in the blasphemous crypt below the cemetery, temporarily melancholy at her absence, but suspecting I had not seen the last of her, and looking forward with an emotion akin to optimism at the thought of the next time I would wake beside her, the warm sunlight from my Montmartre window falling across us.

A Billion Souls Gaze West

Most terrifying hour, day or night:
the dwindling rays of solar light.
No peace, no bliss, no love there dwells
within vast roiling solar swells.

Sentient scum of teeming Earth,
constant stream of death and birth.
Creatures new rise from the clay,
immortal, if but for a day.

Each unjustly vain and proud
until its charnel trench is plowed.
All entranced and none perceiving
masters naught, if not deceiving.

Like burning coals, their feral eyes,
echo yonder crimson skies.

SHROUD OF DUST AND DECAY

Paris, 1903

Editor's Preface

The following narrative consists of excerpts from the diary of Monsieur Adolphe Vaillancourt, late of Paris, covering the period from May 1 to May 20, 1903. This unusual (some would say fantastical) document was part of a large lot of books from Vaillancourt's personal library that were recently purchased at auction in London. In transcribing the selected entries, I made no changes other than corrections to grammar, spelling, and punctuation.

The reader should bear in mind that this document was written "on the fly" with no eye to publication. Vaillancourt's only intent in making these notes was to create a contemporary record of dramatic events he experienced during an extremely trying period in his life. I offer the document without interpretation and make no claims as to its veracity. I believe it speaks for itself.

The Diary of Adolphe Vaillancourt

MAY 1, 1903. It was with unease, even dread, that I ventured out earlier this evening, just after dark fell, descending from the relative safety of my studio on the hilltop village of Montmartre to the chaotic uncertainty of Paris below. In the past few months, I have done such a thing only twice, and both instances proved stressful, and beyond that, potentially dangerous. Under normal circumstances, it would be ludicrous for a grown man to harbor a fear of the dark, but these are not normal circumstances I find myself in, and it is not the darkness itself that terrorizes me; rather, it is those nameless, hideous things that emerge at night from the subterranean realms of Paris. What compelled me to undertake a nocturnal outing despite my reservations was the opening of a one-man show by my dear friend, the painter Maxwell De Russy, at the Xoth gallery on Boulevard St. Germain in the Latin Quarter. Max was counting on me to be there, and I could not in good conscience disappoint him. He knew nothing of the hazards I faced in attending this event, and I saw nothing to be gained by burdening him with the unpleasant facts of the situation.

A small group of us Montmartre artists had planned to meet in front of F. Farr's junk shop on *rue des* Martyres, from whence we would travel to the show together. Although it was but a few blocks from my studio, I felt quite vulnerable making my way along the dark lanes on top of the butte to the upper station of the Montmartre Funicular railway where I rode the railcar down to the foot of the butte and then walked the short distance to the meeting place.

My friends were waiting for me at the junk shop, which was dark inside, being locked for the night. They included Max, his girlfriend, Adelaide, the Spanish painter Santiago L'Espanaye, and the Dutch sculptor Broos Müller. With a bellowing laugh,

Santiago slapped me on the back as he chided me for making them all late. From the shop, we strolled to the Anvers Metro station, bought tickets, and took the Line 2 car to the North station, where we transferred to a Line 1 car. We rode that as far as the Hôtel de Ville, where we climbed off, exited the station, and ascended the stairs into a gas-lit Right Bank district. Max took up a collection from among our group and hired one of the new automobile taxicabs to drive the lot of us across the Seine and into the Latin Quarter. The driver of the noisy contraption deposited us on the sidewalk right outside the gallery where several men in top hats and long frocks stood about smoking cigars.

Inside, the gallery was crowded and warm to the point of being hot. I was happy to see there was a good turnout for Max's show. Indeed, it was standing room only at the front of the gallery where the paintings were hung. I studied the art, nodded to a few acquaintances, and then went in search of a less crowded area where I might breathe more easily. Pressing through the mass of fashionably attired attendees, I eventually found some open space in a back room where drinks were being served. I accepted a glass of white wine from the hostess and loitered around that area, casually examining portions of the establishment that had been left open—or at least were visible—to members of the public. One of these was a storage room off a hallway that apparently doubled as the gallery owner's office. Farther down the hall was a second, more secluded storage area equipped with a sink and toilet. Although the doors to both these rooms were open and no one was telling me to stay out, they bore the feel of private areas that the management likely would consider off-limits to non-employees, had they given it any thought.

Not wanting to draw undue attention to myself by poking around further in places I didn't belong, I meandered back toward the front of the gallery. As I did so, I noticed an oddly recessed space to my left where the main portion of the wall that

37

held art works ended and a second, more crudely constructed wall enclosing the rear of the gallery began. This hollow space was about three feet wide and three feet deep. Stepping into it on a whim, I discovered there was a narrow passageway to my immediate right, extending off into darkness. Due to the angles involved, this passageway had been completely invisible to me before I had stepped into the recess. Curious as to where it might lead, I slowly entered this tunnel-like corridor, hesitantly feeling my way forward with my fingertips tracing along the walls on both sides. Now, I too was hidden from the gallery crowd within this mysterious passageway. When I had gone about fifteen feet, I arrived at a corner that made a sharp turn left, depositing me in a small, gloomily lit chamber that for some reason had the solemn, somber air of a chapel. Before me, at the back of the room, hung heavy black curtains. As I stepped deeper into the chamber, the curtains parted—seemingly on their own—revealing another dimly lit corridor behind the curtains which had roughly hewn stone walls and appeared to be of great age.

Until this point, I had been mildly amused by the almost whimsical nature of this strange section of the building which lay hidden beyond the recess in the wall, but now I grew alarmed and then was practically paralyzed by a sudden, mounting thrill of panic, for I realized that I was leaving the relative safety and normalcy of the gallery and entering an unknown and possibly perilous space—one that might be connected in unwholesome ways with the nefarious lower regions of the city's ancient foundations—the domain of wicked and unfathomable abominations. Before I could give this unsettling idea much thought, an eerie apparition suddenly appeared before me, floating midair in the uncertain darkness immediately past the drawn curtains. It was the naked, luminous, glistening white body of a giant mollusk, floating suspended, its head pointing downward, the tail pointing upward.

Its effect on me was hypnotic; I instantly and unaccountably felt completely at ease, as if a wave of warm, calming water had washed over me, dissolving my visceral fears and negating my rational apprehensions. Not only did I suddenly feel it would be perfectly safe for me to enter this murky chamber and to approach the strange entity suspended before me, which seemed to soundlessly call out to me; I was now irresistibly compelled to respond obediently to what I began to sense was its profound psychic influence on me. Oblivious to any threats to my personal well-being, I lurched forward almost deliriously, staggering blindly toward the obscenely fleshy thing, as it simultaneously drew away—still hanging miraculously suspended in the air with no visible means of support—so that rather than reaching it, I slavishly followed it into the horrid darkness, toward what ultimate end I did not know.

That was the last thing I remembered until I woke up hours later, slumped in a chair in the combination storage room and office that I'd peeked into earlier in the evening. The gallery was now dark, and, from the silence about me, likely empty. The art show was over, the guests had gone home, or—in case of my friends—had progressed to a late dinner and numerous rounds of drinks. The owner had locked up and left, apparently without finding me in his office.

Disturbing questions plagued my mind. What was the gargantuan slug-like creature which had occultly materialized in the corridor beyond the black curtains, and to what unholy rites had it led me within the surrounding unhallowed crypts? What transpired in the hours between that uncanny moment when I began to follow it and my return to consciousness in the gallery owner's office? I had no answers. There was nothing left for me to do but go home.

Although the front doors required a key to exit, I found a side door which opened from the inside without a key and locked itself behind me as I left the gallery. There were no carriages running at that hour, and I was forced to walk the entire distance to the nearest Metro station, where I caught a train back to Montmartre. By the time I finally reached home, it was early morning, dawn's rosy glow clinging to the city's skyline, and I collapsed on the bed, fully dressed, and fell into a dreamless slumber.

MAY 2, 1903. I awoke at noon, exhausted, but too mentally agitated to continue sleeping. Hastily changing into fresh clothes, I walked to the café at the end of my street and had breakfast with several cups of strong black coffee. As I was finishing my eggs and sausage, Santiago came in, saw me, and sat at my table.

"Ah, there you are, my friend! You really gave us the slip last night. What young lady lured you away? That's what we all decided, that you were seduced by one of the tempting models who frequent such festivities."

"There was no young lady. You know I'm married, Santiago."

"Married, but separated, no?"

"Unfortunately, that is the case. Although we no longer live together, I remain faithful to Malora. After all, she is my dear wife, and the mother of my children. I honor that. There are no young women for me, nor any mature ladies."

"I'm sorry to hear that, my friend. A man becomes lonely."

"He does. But I am not entirely alone in this world. There is someone who visits now and then, but we are not lovers in the common sense of the word. As odd as it may sound, she acts as my spiritual adviser."

Santiago perked up, his curiosity piqued. "Do I know this woman?"

"I doubt it. She is known to very few in Montmartre. A reclusive being, who passes though society largely unobserved."

"Now you have my interest. What is her name?"

"Her name—if I can believe what she tells me—is Azrael."

"That is an unusual name. It has a biblical ring to it. What does it mean?"

"She says it means 'Angel of Death.' Or, it can mean 'Help that arrives.' I met her in an ancient church in the Latin Quarter shortly after I fled La Maison de la Limace in horror. I told you about that terrible day, how I could not remain living with Malora and the children. Azrael has helped me deal with the trouble that has plagued me since that day."

"I am aware of this trouble. I see it in your eyes, constantly, and you speak of it on occasion, in a guarded way, but you never explain it in any detail, never say exactly what it entails."

"That's because I do not understand it myself, Santiago, and were I to describe it to you in plain, simple language, you would think me deranged, for I would be speaking with the voice of madness, and yet, this trouble truly exists. It is quite real, and it burdens my very existence."

"Pardon my asking, but do you sleep with this woman?"

I smiled at my friend. His view of life was based purely on the physical; that's where his mind returned to, time after time. "Literally speaking, I suppose I do. For often, that is how our meetings begin: with me awakening to find her lying beside me on my bed in the studio. But all we do is talk. There's no carnal relationship—at least that I'm aware of."

"All right. I had to ask. I understand."

"I hope you do. Like I said, she serves as my spiritual advisor. She helps me fend off malignant forces that seek to ensnare me. And, she has taught me valuable ways to defend myself from occult attack. I should have followed her advice last night when I went out and became separated from our group. I lowered my guard and unwittingly allowed myself to be vulnerable to this predatory phenomenon. I suppose I'm lucky I survived the night, given my foolishness in failing to defend myself."

"What on earth happened?"

41

"I really don't know. Keep this to yourself—it could be dangerous to talk about such things openly, even among our artist friends—but I wandered off within the gallery and found myself in a bizarre back room—a chamber where unholy rituals are seemingly performed—where I saw a most remarkable entity. Some ghastly creature of the night. It resembled a large mollusk, and by large, I mean several feet long. The thing was just hanging in the air in front of me, floating, suspended, and something about it was so weirdly powerful that I could not resist it. I followed it into the depths of the dark chamber, followed it into the night."

"Good lord ..."

"At some point, I lost consciousness, and have no idea from that point forward where I went or what transpired. When I came to, a couple hours later, the gallery was empty, and I was grateful to find myself still alive."

"Was there some way you could have avoided falling under the sway of this monstrous thing?"

"Yes. A technique that Azrael revealed to me. I should have brought along a piece of charcoal in my pocket and marked my forehead with it when I saw the thing, making a protective sigil that she had taught me. I've used the sign on other occasions and so far, it has always worked, but last night I was foolish. It's something of a miracle that I'm here to tell the tale."

Santiago pondered this for a while. "Perhaps last night this thing was not trying to take you by force, to destroy you at that particular moment. Rather, perhaps it was attempting to win you over through some allure it has upon its victims. To gain your heart and mind before it takes your flesh."

"You could be right about that, Santiago. As I said, please keep this in the strictest confidence."

"My lips are sealed."

After talking with Santiago, I went back to the studio and spent the afternoon painting, feeling more peaceful now that I had confided in a trusted friend. It was a lovely day, the sunlight warming the rows of grapevines on the hillside below my window. I began a new egg-tempera painting—a female nude, sprawled on an unmade bed much like the one in my studio. I didn't know who it was meant to represent. Maybe it was supposed to be Azrael, although the figure in my picture was not as severely lean as I knew Azrael to be. But the figure did have Azrael's unusually long torso and limbs, her elongated head, as well as her flat, flaxen-colored hair. The nude's face was somewhat like Azrael's— emaciated, with sunken eyes and cheeks—but its skin tones were a healthier shade of coral, instead of the pale blue hue of my mysterious visitor's flesh, so reminiscent of a corpse's pallor.

Once I started thinking of this painting as being a portrait of Azrael, I couldn't resist the temptation to sketch in an ancient, tattered robe hanging on a nail on the wall behind the figure, like the one Azrael always wore. Privately, I would consider this an idealized image of Azrael, but for the sake of appearances, I officially titled the work *Nude No. 5,* having painted four other nudes recently, although none of them were like this piece in any way. When I laid down my brush for the day, the painting wasn't anywhere near being finished, but it was in a state in which I felt comfortable leaving it. As darkness fell, I cooked my dinner, ate, and went to bed early, still tired from the night before.

MAY 5, 1903. Last night I had a most unusual dream. I was walking along the uppermost streets of Montmartre at night and came to Sacré-Coeur, the recently raised basilica that sits upon the pinnacle of the butte. I entered the church to discover a religious service in progress. The pews were filled with parishioners, and an organist was playing. I found an empty seat in the last row of benches and took it. Each of the parishioners held in their lap a lit votive candle cradled within a small glass vial. The glow of these candles was the only illumination in the church, and it was so dim that I couldn't make out any of the parishioners' faces, hidden as they were within the cowls of their robes. But I did see the gleaming eyes of some of these malignant celebrants, and the sight filled me with dread. Their eyes burned like coals and seethed with malevolence. As the music came to an end, a heavy figure garbed in a purple cloak shot through with golden threads lumbered up to the pulpit and began to read from a folio volume. I did not recognize the crudely guttural language which the priest spoke, nor that of the parishioners who answered his rhythmic calls with equally rhythmic responses. Nonetheless, their barbaric chanting, which increased in volume as it went on until it reached a feverish roar, instilled considerable uneasiness in me.

At that moment, I noticed the priest's robes were bunched up in back, as if some solid appendage that descended tail-like from his body were preventing the fabric from falling all the way to the floor. And I thought I saw a thick, tubular limb extending away from the podium and across the floor to where it disappeared into the shadows behind the altar. Glancing up and down the row in which I was seated, I could see similar appendages coming out from under the robes of the parishioners around me. Despite the dimness of the church interior, these mucus-covered limbs— which seemingly were attached to every person present except me—glistened feebly in the flickering candlelight.

I had seen such a thing before, in an ancient crypt within an abandoned chalk quarry that Azrael and I had entered through the Montmartre cemetery. From a concealed position among the sarcophagi, we had observed an elderly monk who was shambling along between rows of caskets stacked against the walls. Attached to the decrepit body of this accursed man was just such an unnatural limb. Azrael called the entity that had affixed part of itself to this unfortunate person *"La Limace."* In English, the phrase means "The Slug." That, among the entire range of natural creatures, was what this parasitic being most resembled: a slug. I don't know if these things are really members of the Mollusca phylum—if they are gastropods—never having seen the complete body of one. All I've seen so far are their tentacular limbs which maliciously join themselves to human bodies. As in the case of that poor monk; as in the case of Malora.

Indeed, I don't even know if there are multiple living specimens of *La Limace*—if a population of such creatures exists in Paris—or if there is only one such entity with a great many tentacle-like limbs that extend in all directions throughout the city's underground and yet are all appendages leading back to one central corpus.

At that point in the dream, I began to fear for my life. Bolting from my row, climbing over and at times slipping upon the muscular flesh of the slug appendages, I ran to the back of the church and raced up a spiral staircase into the heights of a bell tower. A throng of parishioners gave pursuit. I could hear the hasty treading of their feet upon the stone steps while the collective light from their candles swirled up the stairway walls toward me. I was sure they would catch me and inflict some terrible harm upon me, but somehow, I reached the top of the stairs and emerged onto the open balcony before my pursuers reached me. From this high vantage point, all of Paris lay before me, but there was nowhere for me to go, nowhere to escape to. I prepared to meet my doom, crossing my arms over my chest and closing my eyes. And then, in the kind of miraculous salvation that only occurs in dreams, I heard the wispy voice of Azrael speaking from out of a shadow behind one of the balcony's stone columns.

"Step hither, child, and I will save thee."

I opened my eyes, lowered my arms, and stared into the shadows. She was barely visible, her form a pale radiance that almost blended into the murky gloom behind the column.

"Make haste, for they approach!"

I did as she instructed, stepped forward and felt her long arms enfolding me, and then the gauzy, tattered robe that hung from her shoulders like an angel's gossamer wings wrapped itself tightly around me.

The parishioners at the head of the pack burst onto the balcony, stopping dead in their tracks once they looked all around and saw no trace of me.

At that moment, Azrael and I rose up from the balcony floor and flew out through one of the spaces between columns and into the open air. How this was possible, I do not comprehend. We seemed to be invisible to my attackers, for they did not glance in our direction, although a few of them peered over the balcony railing to see if I had fallen from the great height or jumped to my death.

Bonded together through some agency of spiritual energy or occult science, we soared over the city at a great speed, sometimes swooping down low to a position just above the dome of a cathedral, shrine, or other temple, where we would hover for a few seconds before moving on. Unlike Sacré-Coeur, the holy structures we visited in this way were very ancient, dating from the earliest days of Paris' inhabitation. The night sky was peppered with fleecy white altocumulus clouds, between which brilliant stars twinkled in the blackness of space—a beautiful yet terrifying sight. Finally, we arrive at the old Latin Quarter church where I had first met Azrael some time ago. We set down there on the high balcony of a tower, and Azrael unfolded her arms, freeing me from her protective grasp, as the wing-like folds of her filmy gown fell away, taking their normal position upon her form.

I wanted to ask how she had known that I was in danger and how she was able to lift me from the top of Sacré-Coeur and carry the pair of us through the air for a bird's-eye view of Paris.

"Azrael …"

She stopped me by pressing two of her fingertips against my

lips and whispering "Hush, sweet child. There is no mystery in it, for I am help that arrives, and it is my nature to grant thee sanctuary in times of peril."

At that, the dream faded, and I awoke in bed, lying on my side, facing the open window which looked out upon a scene much like that in the dream, with all of Paris laid out below, but as seen from a less-elevated perspective than in the dream. Across the room, the half-finished painting of Azrael sat propped up on the easel, but in the wash of cool moonlight from the window, her nude form now had a bluish cast to it, making the skin tones more closely resemble Azrael's actual appearance.

It was a remarkable dream—if, in fact, it was a dream. It occurred to me that what I believed to be a nocturnal psychic vision may have been a real, physical experience, fantastical as it was. It was her way to arrive quietly, imperceptibly, while I was sleeping, and I sometimes found her lying beside me, chastely, when I awoke. On reflection, I was not even very surprised by the idea of her being able to fly. Judging from what I'd seen so far, she appeared to be either a supernatural being—a spirit—or a physical creature with profoundly developed supernatural abilities. She was, in a word, magical.

MAY 7, 1903. Santiago dropped by the studio today to see my latest work in progress—the painting I'm calling *Nude No. 5*.

"It is the mysterious lady you spoke of, no?" he asked. It was a perceptive guess, and I confessed that he was right.

"Yes, although I'm making her look more 'normal,' if you will. If I tried to accurately reproduce her real flesh tones, she would look positively cadaverous, like some ghoul that had crawled out of a graveyard. In life, she's extremely pale and very emaciated, which sounds awful, I know, but nonetheless she's quite lovely in a strange way. You have to see her to appreciate her beauty."

"It sounds like perhaps you are in love with this woman."

"In love? Oh, no, but I am quite charmed by her. I can't imagine where she comes from, nor what her history might be. Everything about her is uncommon—she's unlike anyone I've ever known. A complete mystery." I didn't want my friend thinking I was being unfaithful to Malora, even if just emotionally.

He was about to leave when he remembered something in his coat pocket that he had intended to give me: a handbill he had found posted on a bulletin board at Sacré-Coeur. It was an announcement for a talk on occult forces at work in modern day Paris. There was to be a meeting in a small tavern at the base of the hill.

"You should go to this. It's free, tomorrow afternoon. I've heard this speaker before, and he is knowledgeable. He may be able to tell you something about the monstrous entity that you have witnessed on occasion. Maybe he even knows what's up with your mysterious lady friend, Azrael. It can't hurt to ask, eh? It might be worth your time."

I thanked him and said I would consider it, although my instinct was to not confide about such matters with a stranger. Could I trust this man to keep what I said to himself? I didn't want ugly rumors about me and Malora to start spreading through the Marais, alarming our friends and my former business associates.

May 8, 1903. I decided to attend the talk as a silent listener in the back of the room, determined not to approach the speaker nor ask any questions from the audience. That way, I might learn something of the hideous circumstances that I and my family were forced to deal with without sacrificing our privacy.

The speaker's name was Henri de Atal. A portly, well-dressed man in his forties with shoulder-length brown hair and bushy eyebrows, he seemed well-educated if somewhat eccentric. His talk, which lasted an hour, was quite interesting, although had I not already had the experiences that I had, I would have thought much of what he said preposterous. To my surprise, the topics he discussed included *La Limace,* along with other local manifestations of the occult, devoting fifteen minutes to the subject. He went into considerable detail, but here is the gist of what he said:

- *La Limace* may be but a single creature, rather than many individual creatures. Authorities disagree on this point.
- Its limbs have spread themselves throughout Paris.
- The ends of the limbs rise above ground level and enter homes and other buildings from a vast subterranean network where they are all connected to a central body.
- The location of this central body has not yet been discovered, although researchers have been gathering clues to its whereabouts for years.
- *La Limace* has been in Paris for centuries, with mentions of it appearing in certain pre-Roman writings.
- It is a malignant entity that preys upon humans and is parasitic in nature, extracting nutrients and "life energy" from its victims, who suffer greatly from the relationship.
- Victims have their vitality slowly drained away over many years, ultimately becoming walking corpses, their minds and bodies entirely under the sway of "the great slug," as he called it.
- Early in the process, victims become reclusive, withdrawing to the lowest levels accessible to them in whatever structure they inhabit, and thereafter seldom venture up to higher levels as the corruption of their body progresses.

Thus far, I accepted everything he said as plausible, much of it being consistent with what I had already seen or suspected. But then he made a claim that I found very hard to accept:

- When the parasitic contagion is greatly advanced, the victim becomes encased in a cocoon-like growth (he called it a "shroud") that forms at the end of the entity's

49

extended limb. Within this shell, the victim's body undergoes a marked transformation as it enters a new life stage. The victim ceases to be human and becomes a new type of creature. Once fully developed, this creature emerges from the cocoon and breaks away from the slug's control, physically and mentally. It flees the subterranean nest that *La Limace* has created and takes on a life independent of the slug, abandoning all aspects of its former existence as a human being.

That part was too farfetched, too extreme for me to accept. I wouldn't believe it unless I saw it with my own eyes.

On my way out after the meeting broke up, I ran into Gregor, our old maintenance man. He was seated at a table by the door, nursing the remains of a coffee. Seeing him brought an unexpected swelling of emotion to my breast. I greatly missed my former life at La Maison and anything reminiscent of those happier days was both precious and painful to me.

"May I join you, Gregor?"

"But of course, sir." He pulled out a chair for me.

"Thank you. How is the situation at home—any better?"

"No, sir. Even worse than before, I'm afraid. My deep concern for the well-being of Madame Malora is what has brought me here today. I picked up a leaflet announcing the talk after Mass last week at Notre Dame and thought that perhaps Monsieur de Atal would address how one might dispel the pest from a home. But as you know, he did not talk about ways in which a victim may be liberated—only the bare facts of their oppression. And now there are so many people gathered around him, asking questions, offering their own stories, that I doubt I will have a chance to converse with the man today."

"I'd rather you didn't, anyway, Gregor. This matter is sensitive—best kept confidential, and not spread outside the family. Possibly what we've learned today can guide us in further research as to what may be done. Perhaps the information we seek has been published and may be found in a library or bookshop, without our having to reveal unpleasant details to strangers who may not have our best interests in mind. I'm very glad I ran into you, Gregor. I've been considering paying a visit to La Maison and may want to enlist your assistance when I do."

"Certainly, sir. I'm at your full disposal. All you need do is to alert me when you plan to come, and I will be prepared for it."

"Excellent." We shook hands good-bye. "It's delightful seeing you again. Do take care." He wished me well in return.

MAY 11, 1903. This afternoon I finished *Nude No. 5* and then indulged myself with a much-needed nap, having been up late the night before reading a volume of Parisian occult lore that I'd bought in a bookshop near the Luxembourg Gardens the day before. A slender volume in a decaying calfskin binding, the book contained several references to "the Beast under Place des Vosges," one of which told of an effort by residents in the early 1830s to exterminate the creature. That effort was largely unsuccessful, although it had succeeded in driving the monster to withdraw to lower levels of the building's substructure. Unfortunately, the book didn't state exactly what measures the residents had taken in their attack on the Beast, other than that it was a combination of "Romani Magic" and "brute force." Exhausted as I was, I fell into a deep sleep that would have lasted beyond my usual dinnertime, had I not been abruptly awakened by the sensation that I was not alone in bed. A form that was as feminine as Malora's was pressing against my back, although unlike my wife's body, it lacked normal human warmth, and at the same time I detected a hint of breath on the nape of my neck. Startled, I sat up and turned to face my visitor.

"Oh, it's you, Azrael. I wasn't sure I would see you again. It's been a while."

51

"Nay, 'tis more recent than ye think," she said in a breathless whisper. "Not so long ago, I came to thy aid in the bell tower. Surely ye recall?"

"I do, but I thought that was merely a dream."

"It was no dream. Thy spirit travelled to Sacré-Coeur, to witness those who pay homage to *La Limace*. Those acolytes attacked thee, and would have done thee great harm, had I not taken thee away through the air."

"I thought it seemed too real for a dream. How did you know I was there?"

"I watch over thee without cease and protect thee every hour. That is my nature."

"Then I am very lucky."

"'Tis not luck but ordained."

I arose from bed, walked to the easel, and looked back at Azrael for her reaction to my portrait of her. "What do you think? Have I faithfully captured your spirit?"

"As I am seen by men, yea, although much about me remains unseen."

"You must know what I'm planning to do."

"I do."

"Then tell me how I may succeed."

"Proceed with caution and use what I have taught thee."

"You mean to make the mark on my forehead with soot?"

"Indeed. *La Limace* may not approach while you bear the mark."

"I will do that. I was foolish not to have it on me at the basilica that night. And even more so when I entered that passageway at the art gallery. You were there as well?"

She nodded *Yes*. "It was I who interceded in the ceremony and brought you to the room where you later awakened."

"I should have known as much. So, that night at the gallery, the weird mollusk I saw suspended in midair, that I followed down the dark corridor, was that thing somehow related to *La Limace?*"

"It was."

There was more I wanted to ask her, but I was suddenly overcome with drowsiness. Stumbling back to the bed, I lay down beside her. She brushed an errant lock of hair from my eyes as a mother would do to a child, then rose from the bed and walked over to the table by the easel. Opening her gown and exposing her bare breasts—which were full and not shriveled by decrepitude, as I would have expected, given her otherwise cadaverous appearance—she took from a sling that hung about her waist an ancient sword in a scabbard. Holding it at arm's length before her, the tip pointed upward, she stated "The Blade of the Saint severs the flesh of the Beast. Take it with thee to thy former home. It will separate thy loved one from the corruption."

Then she turned and laid the sword on the table with a clank, picked up a paint brush, rubbed its tip in a puddle of red pigment on the palette, and began to make brush strokes on my painting, but my eyes shut themselves against my will before I could see what she was painting, and I fell into a deep sleep. Later, when I awakened, she was gone.

I rose up and examined the altered canvas. She had written a symbol of some sort across the image of her face in the portrait. It was similar in style to the sigil she had taught me to inscribe on my forehead to ward off *La Limace,* but not identical to it. I didn't know what it meant, but decided to leave it there, as it was—a part of the finished painting.

The sword was shorter than a full-sized battle weapon. More like a long dagger. It appeared to be hundreds of years old, if not a thousand. Its blade was decorated with figures that had been etched into the hardened steel, while the cast silver scabbard was covered in figures of men and animals. It looked as if it belonged in a museum. I hid it securely in my studio before going to bed that night.

53

May 12, 1903. I telephoned Gregor to say I would be at the house tomorrow afternoon at 3 o'clock, and to make ready. We agreed to meet at the cafe in the ground floor arcade that circles the building, at what had been my favorite table when I lived there.

May 13, 1903. I left Montmartre an hour before our appointment to allow time for travel. Walked to Anvers station, took Metro Line 2 to North station, transferred to Line 1, and hopped off at Hôtel de Ville. From there, I walked east along the arcades of *rue de* Rivoli to the Hôtel de Sully, turned north and passed through the hotel grounds, and arrived at Place des Vosges. The Place is shabbier than it was when I moved out. More empty apartments with "To Let" notices on their doors. An air of abandonment and small signs of neglect in the building's maintenance. Fewer merchants in the arcades, and of a lower order. A grocer's stand selling cabbages has taken over the shadowy corner near the door to La Maison de la Limace.

I wore my long coat to conceal the sword that Azrael had given me, which hung from a belt around my waist. In one pocket was the loaded service revolver I had borrowed from Santiago (I did not share my plans with him, saying only that I was going into a dangerous situation and might need to defend myself), in the other, a charcoal stick for making a sigil on my forehead, should it come to that. Also hidden under the coat, tucked into my belt, was the rolled-up canvas of my painting *Nude No. 5,* which I had removed from its stretcher, as instructed by Azrael in a dream the night before. I found Gregor at a café table in the arcade, as planned. He insisted that I sit and refresh myself before we began, so I ordered a coffee from the waiter. Gregor was visibly agitated—clearly apprehensive concerning the actions we were about to take.

"Do not feel you are obligated to participate in this," I told him. "If you will simply admit me into the apartment and then go about your normal workday, I will consider it a great act of friendship."

"But, sir, that would not be an honorable way for me to act. I insist on joining you in this mission, no matter what the risks."

"We could perish, Gregor. Challenging that monstrosity may be our last deed."

"Then so be it, sir. At least we will die as men of valor."

Soon my cup was empty and there was no excuse for further delaying the inevitable. Leaving a generous tip, I rose and followed Gregor to La Maison.

"I suggest we enter by the main door and not the cellar, even though the latter is likely closer to where we'll eventually find Malora and the children," I said. "I want to examine the upstairs rooms of the apartment first, before we begin the hunt for *La Limace* in the areas below."

Gregor unlocked the apartment entryway from the arcade, and we walked up one floor. Although I'd spent countless hours in these rooms over the years and nothing had physically changed since I'd left in a panic a year ago, it all felt radically different now. The apartment seemed abandoned, like a home that is returned to after a long trip. The essence of this impression was that no living thing had occupied these spaces on a continuous basis for some time, other than spiders and mice, and now, here we were, disturbing that terrible stillness and silence. Of course, the maids had done their regular housekeeping—the floors had been washed and the furniture dusted—but they had not stayed very long at any one time, and the gloom of desertion hung in the airless rooms.

With Gregor a few steps behind me, I perfunctorily strode through the series of rooms that one first encounters off the second-floor landing—the parlor, the drawing room, the dining room—only stopping when we reached the ballroom. Seeing it again brought an unexpected swelling of emotion to my breast, a nostalgia for the early days of our courtship. It was in this room that I first laid eyes on Malora. She was conversing with three other young ladies, all of them dressed in finery appropriate for the occasion—a festive dance to which the family's many friends and business associates had been invited, myself included. That was before *La Limace* had laid claim to her soul, when she was still a woman of free will, and radiant with youthful vitality. I fell in love with her on the spot. Would that I could return to that moment, sweep her away into the night, and flee Paris forever, escaping the curse of the thing that dwelt below La Maison de la Limace. But there had been no way I could have foreseen what lay ahead for us. The peril was not obvious at first. All seemed well during that blissful hour, with the guests sipping their champagne and making merry. How could I have known of the sinister influence that lay in wait for us, the fiendish thing that would prey on our spirits, and on her very flesh, in the years that followed?

"Too much time has passed since there has been dancing and merriment in this room," Gregor lamented.

"Or laughter in any of these rooms," I added.

We moved on. The rest of the apartment—the kitchen, the scullery, the two bedchambers, my study, the water closet—all were equally lifeless and unwelcoming in their strange quietness.

"There is nothing to see here, Gregor. We must go below."

There are two ways to descend downstairs from the apartment: through an exterior door out on the arcade that leads down a stone stairway, or from inside the apartment, down wooden stairs entered from the back hallway. Both connect with a brick-lined passageway that is the only way in and out of the cellar. Gregor has a crowded little workshop off to one side of the arcade entrance foyer. I asked if we could stop in there first before we went down, to retrieve a hammer and tacks.

"I want to post this at the cellar doorway," I said, removing the canvas from under my coat and unrolling it.

"What is the purpose of that, sir?"

"As a talisman. It will prevent *La Limace* from passing through the cellar and into the apartment from below." Gregor's expression indicated that he had trouble believing this claim. "I have it on good authority," I explained, "that it will protect Malora and the children—if we succeed in bringing them up today."

He fetched the hammer and tacks, and we went down the stone stairs and into the dank brick passageway, following it a short distance to the cellar's arched doorway, where we stopped.

"Here," I said, positioning the flattened-out painting of Azrael on the arch's column at about eye-level. Gregor tacked it up, his face still contorted with doubt about the efficacy of this intended magic. "The beast will be unable to pass this image," I said, "which it will find excruciatingly painful to observe."

"I suppose that may be possible. We know so little of this creature and its ways."

We performed a hasty search of the several small rooms comprising the cellar, finding nothing unusual, as expected.

"It, and my family, must be in the spaces below, assuming they are still at this location and haven't been moved by the creature. Please lead the way, Gregor. You're more familiar with these lower regions than I am."

"Certainly, sir."

At this point I drew the service revolver from my coat pocket. Gregor saw it but said nothing. The chambers below the cellar were built in the early Middle Ages, and were cruder in construction, showing fewer signs of modern usage. We came to the end of the area that had artificial lighting and began using our lanterns to illuminate the path. The network of rooms, corridors, and stairs quickly became maze-like, and I would have been entirely lost without Gregor to guide me. He seemed to know where he was going.

In one particularly primitive passageway that was flooded with three or four inches of foul water, Gregor abruptly halted. Inhaling deeply, he grimaced and whispered to me: "We are drawing near. I detect the fetid odor of the slug." He ran the beam of his lantern along one wall of the ancient passageway, then up the opposing wall, stopping it at a narrow door into a side room. Keeping the beam focused there, he whispered back to me, "In there, perhaps. We should approach with caution."

Again, I allowed him to take the lead, bringing out my own lantern so that I would be able to see in the event we became separated during an attack.

At this location, I noticed traces of a slimy, mucus-like substance on the walls—a greasy, translucent slime left behind by the appendages of *La Limace* as it repeatedly explored the upper areas and then retreated.

Gregor tenuously entered the pitch-dark side room, with me a few feet behind. Running our lanterns over the walls and floor, we soon learned that this room was empty, but it held another doorway into a deeper space. Gregor entered that space and again, I followed. This chamber, in turn, was likewise empty, but led into yet another room, which, unlike the rooms we had just passed through, was faintly lit by some weak light source coming through the doorway from still another room. Curious as to what was giving off this pale, yellow light, we stepped into this latest chamber and saw, in one corner, a flickering candle stump set on a ceramic plate. I immediately recognized the decorative pattern of the plate; it was from a set of fine dinnerware that Malora had inherited from her mother years ago.

This chamber showed signs of recent habitation. A filthy quilt was haphazardly spread upon the floor near the candle. Children's toys were strewn about the room. One of these I recognized: a miniature wooden rocking horse that belonged to my seven-year-old second daughter, Maria.

"We are almost there!" whispered Gregor, an urgent note of excitement in his voice. Suddenly he thrust up a hand to stop me from replying, and we both listened intently. A small, frail voice could be heard, coming from somewhere far off. A child was speaking in a rhythmic manner, then began to sing a familiar nursery rhyme.

"Maria!" I called out. "It's Father! Come to me! I am by the candle."

Her singing stopped.

"Daddy?"

"Yes! I'm here to bring you back into the light, to our home. Come quickly, to the room with the candle and blanket."

As an aside to Gregor, I whispered, "Do you think this is the nursery, where the children stay?"

He shook his head *No*. "Apparently, it's an outlying room sometimes used by the children, which suggests that the nursery proper may be close by. And the nursery is surely adjacent to the crypt occupied by *La Limace*. A strong odor will tell us when we have reached the nursery. It has the foul stench of an animal's den—that's the smell of *La Limace*. The slug is clever at hiding and can move about quickly, but it can't conceal its telltale stink."

The sound of small, bare feet running toward us echoed in the air, and an instant later, Maria burst through a dark doorway in the back wall and into the chamber. She threw her arms about my legs, crying, "Daddy, daddy, daddy!"

"It's okay, darling; everything is going to be okay. Where are your mother and brother and sisters?"

She pointed to the doorway from which she had just emerged.

"In there," she whimpered, "with the *thing*."

"I know about the *thing*, Maria, and I will not permit it to keep you children and your mother down here any longer. Gregor and I aim to banish it from this home forever."

"Allow me, sir, to go on alone to find the others," said Gregor, his lantern trained on the doorway into deeper realms where *La Limace* dwelt. "You should stay behind to protect Maria. She will not be safe without one of us guarding her."

I loathed allowing him to face the menace alone, but I hated more the idea of leaving Maria defenseless now that we had found her. "All right, but please take this," I said, handing him the revolver. "We don't know if it will stop the slug, but it's worth a try if the thing attacks you."

"Thank you, sir." He tucked the pistol into his belt and walked into the darkness through the doorway.

At this stage, events become uncertain in my memory—it all happened so quickly. I watched anxiously as Gregor penetrated deeper and deeper into the darkness. I could follow his progress thanks to the beam of his lantern which lit up his immediate surroundings. He quickly passed through a small chamber and then entered a long, straight corridor. From what I could see at that distance, this was more a rough-hewn tunnel that had been cut through solid stone than a formal passageway built of bricks and mortar. Next, I heard two voices: a young girl and a toddler. They were sobbing hysterically, or perhaps what I heard were their manic expressions of joy at being rescued, and I distinctly heard the older child say, "Gregor." Then the silhouettes of the two children broke away from Gregor's silhouette and ran—as one figure—toward me. When they were close enough to appear in the beam of my lantern, I saw that it was my oldest daughter, eight-year-old Samantha, carrying in her arms our youngest child, the two-year-old Rachel. A moment later, the pair of them ran into the chamber where Maria and I awaited, and we were reunited.

Gregor loudly called back to me, "I believe your son is immediately ahead, sir."

"Excellent, Gregor! Speak no further, lest you attract the thing."

I saw him nodding that he understood, then he turned and walked deeper into the tunnel. It was maddening, waiting for my boy to be found. What seemed like a long while passed, and although I saw a silhouette that was probably Gregor's far away in the depths of the tunnel, I couldn't make out much detail.

"Listen," I said to my daughters. "You three stay right here. Do not enter that door! I'm going in a little way to see if Gregor needs my help. I'll be close enough that I can come right back if anything happens. You'll be safe here."

And I didn't go very deep into the tunnel. Just enough so that I could make out what Gregor was doing. Every few seconds, I turned around to make sure the girls were still there and not being threatened by anything. Once, glancing at them, I realized all three were filthy, as if they hadn't bathed or changed clothes in weeks. This made me wonder if they were no longer being cared for by the servants. I made a mental note to investigate that question later.

After a long silence, I heard a new voice: that of my four-year-old son, William. He was speaking to Gregor in a calm voice, but I couldn't make out his exact words. Then he walked past Gregor and came toward me down the dark tunnel. When he stepped into the light of my lantern, I was shocked at his condition. Like his sisters, he was dirty and disheveled, with a dazed look on his face. That was surely the result of his being held captive by *La Limace*. He came the rest of the way and calmly leaned his head against my leg but said nothing.

"Willy, join your sisters in the room behind me, where the candle burns. You'll be safe there. I'll be right here, where I can see you. I want to watch Gregor bring out your mother."

"Mother is different now," he said in a flat voice. "She's with the bad thing."

"We'll help free her from it. Now join your sisters."

He walked away in silence.

61

That's when something very strange, but not altogether unfamiliar to me, happened. Out of the depths of the dark tunnel beyond Gregor emerged a bizarre creature very similar to the one I had seen at the art gallery that night. I had since learned from Azrael that this repulsive entity—which she called "The Terrible Infant"—was of the same species as *La Limace,* but it was at an earlier stage in the creature's life cycle. An immature *Limace.* She had warned me against the *Enfant.* It sought to lure unsuspecting persons into congress with *La Limace* and must be avoided. On rare occasions, an *Enfant* would consume the body of a human and begin its transformation into a mature Limace. As before, the creature's slimy, gelatinous body miraculously floated in midair, suspended with no visible means of support, its long, tapered form oriented vertically, with its supposed "head" pointing down and its "tail" pointing up. This monstrosity was no more than ten feet from Gregor when I first detected it. After a brief hesitation, the abominable thing rushed toward Gregor. Seeing no alternative course of action, Gregor raised the pistol and immediately fired a loud series of shots that reverberated throughout the underground complex, but to no effect. The bullets didn't stop it. The thing, which was about a foot wide and three feet long, tightly wrapped itself around Gregor's head, covering his face and quickly smothering his screams of terror. The pistol drooped in his hand, his arms and legs went limp, and he was dragged off into the dark recesses of the tunnel by the still floating monster.

"Gregor!" I screamed. "Good God, man, fight it with all you have!" But there was nothing to be done. Seconds later, the muted echoes of his agonized cries reached me from what sounded like a great distance. Somewhere within the depths of the vast network of ancient crypts below La Maison de la Limace, Gregor met his death. Knowing that his fate was sealed and that I was unable to save him, I turned away from this good friend and loyal servant and ran back to the candlelit room where I hastily marked the children's foreheads with sigils to protect them from the wiles of the slug, and I marked myself as well. Then I went to find Malora and hopefully to rescue her, God willing.

Would I perish like Gregor? I pondered my odds. The service revolver was gone, having been carried away by Gregor, but it had proven useless against these things anyway, so that really was not much of a loss. To my advantage, I still had the "Blade of the Saint"—the magical sword, which according to Azrael would be a powerful weapon against *La Limace*. Now I was about to trust my life to the might of this ancient blade, along with the arcane symbol marked in soot on my brow.

The tunnel before me was more primitive than anything we had encountered to that point, descending into unknown blackness at a severe angle. Penetrating it, I began to see lining the walls various pieces of old furniture that someone, or something, had brought down from the cellar above where they had been stored. A few of the pieces I recognized, although many I did not. A mahogany bureau came into view, one drawer half pulled out, dingy white linen petticoats spilling forth. Other articles of clothing were strewn across the floor—including children's garments as well as personal items that belonged to Malora. I saw the once-lovely gown she had worn the first time I met her; it was a violation of all that is holy for it to be so disrespectfully treated. The foul odor in the air was becoming much stronger; I was nearing the nest; of that I was certain. The film of dried slime coating the walls was thicker here, bearing witness to repeated rubbings by the limbs of *La Limace*. A few copper pots from our scullery had been discarded in a murky corner, the rotted remains of an unidentifiable meal encrusting them.

The walls curved outward as I progressed, and the tunnel opened into a broader cave-like chamber. Soon I began to see mounds of brown, detached skulls and stacks of old bones, along with morbidly carved stone sarcophagi. I soon realized that I was in one of the subterranean crypts below Place des Vosges that I had often heard stories about, and further, that the so-called "nest" where *La Limace* had been holding my family captive was likely located within this very crypt. My beloved children and wife had been living a macabre shadow existence among the remains of the ancient dead. My soul was struck with profound horror in response to this blasphemous knowledge, but I had no time to dwell on that, for suddenly before me in the feeble glare of the lantern beam stood an appalling apparition: my own true darling, the love of my life, the formerly beautiful and now horrific apparition of Malora.

She looked more dead than alive. Her emaciated face and the wrinkled backs of her hands were the pale, unhealthy ivory of a cadaver's cold white skin. Her formerly glossy raven black hair was now lusterless, dirty, and dull—dusky without sheen. The crimson satin gown she was garbed in was tattered at the hem and shamefully threadbare. Worst of all, her eyes were rolled up into her skull, revealing only the expressionless whites.

I cried out in anguish at the terrible sight of her.

In possible response, Malora croaked an unintelligible utterance—her voice dry and raspy. Then she twitched all over, as if suddenly recognizing my voice and becoming aware of my unexpected presence. I reached out gently to take her hand, intending to escort her from this hellish scene, but she jerked it away violently, and drew back from me, moving oddly, as if her body were being pulled away from behind.

Using more force this time, I grabbed her roughly by the upper arm and twisted her around, exposing her back, which previously had been hidden from my view.

And God help me, that's when I saw the awful reality of the situation, something I had only suspected before: the end of the gigantic slug's long tentacular appendage coiling up from the floor behind her and entering a raggedly torn opening in her gown at the small of her back. I savagely ripped away a large portion of the gown's fabric and saw this abomination: the thick stump of the creature's appendage entering her body, its blue-tinted tissues having grown into—and in areas blended with—Malora's precious flesh.

The revulsion that welled up in my gut ignited within me an extreme rage, a burning hatred for *La Limace,* and I acted as a wild animal would, without rational deliberation. I do not recall drawing the sword from its scabbard, only the moment when the blade struck and sliced through the monster's meaty limb, engaging and overpowering sturdy muscle and sinew, and severing the connection between it and she. The beast's high-pitched squeals filled the air, and the detached portion of the appendage withdrew wildly, disappearing into the shadows that lay beyond my lantern's light. I heard the thunderous commotion of the creature's sudden retreat, its mutilated tentacle slithering away from us, banging against monuments and cavern walls as it withdrew. In shock from this abrupt alteration to her physical being, Malora passed out, collapsing into my arms. Still clenching the wetted sword in one hand and the lantern in the other, I carried her away to where the children waited, then led them all back up to the surface level, not resting until we had passed the column where Gregor and I had posted the marked canvas that would deter an intrusion by the creature. I knew that *La Limace* was only temporarily defeated, wounded but not mortally so, and soon would attempt to find another way into the apartment, intent on again enslaving my family and wreaking vengeance on me.

But for a while it would be stopped by the cryptic red symbol that Azrael had brushed upon the painting. The creature could not progress beyond that sanctified image; Azrael would not allow it.

This evening, reflecting on what had happened down in the crypt, I realized that I had seen two extraordinary things in the dimly lit grey field of countless tombs arrayed behind Malora as I struck the blow that freed her from the creature. The first was that I had caught a faint glimpse of Azrael watching me from the shadows. I had perceived her at the edge of my field of vision, but it didn't fully register at the time. I am certain this was no illusion. She had been watching over us, protecting us from the ravenous evil of *La Limace*. The second thing I had seen was the outline of the creature itself, looming behind the clustered mausoleums: the massive, shell-less body of an alien entity that only superficially resembled a gargantuan gastropod mollusk but could not be any such thing in reality. A brief glint of lantern light had been reflected off its colossal flank, and then I detected a leering stare from the bulbous eyespots on the ends of the feelers extending from the creature's head. *La Limace* was bigger and more horrific than I ever could have imagined.

MAY 14, 1903. Immediately after the rescue yesterday I sent one of the servants to fetch our family physician. We have known him for many years, and he can be trusted to keep what he saw confidential. The good news is that no lasting harm was done to the children. *La Limace* did not interact with them physically, although it did seem to have exerted some degree of psychic control over them. Now that they are removed from proximity to the creature, its mental influence is dissipating, and the doctor is confident they soon will be restored to a normal state of mind.

The same cannot be said of Malora. For several years, her flesh was bonded to and interlaced with the creature's flesh, and many of her human biological processes were—according to the doctor—radically compromised. He performed emergency surgery on her yesterday afternoon, closing the wound on her back where the creature's tentacle had entered her body, after cutting away as much of the alien tissue as was possible. Surprisingly, she suffered little blood loss before and during the surgery; possibly, he speculated, because her heartbeat was slowed and her circulation in a suppressed state due to being attached to the creature for so long. Regrettably, the unhealthily desiccated condition of her skin may not be reversible; the creature has, in the doctor's words, "sucked the life fluids from her." And yet, she survives. Weak, mentally distant, pale of complexion, but alive.

MAY 15, 1903. The help, who understandably made themselves scarce during the prolonged absence of Malora and the children, are now constantly about the apartment—cleaning, cooking, chattering, and no doubt gossiping amongst themselves about the uncanny events in La Maison de la Limace. I have spoken with each of them privately and am convinced that they performed their duties as well as could be expected, given the unusual circumstances. I explained to them the unfortunate loss of Gregor and gained their assurance they would not divulge details about his presumed death to curious outsiders. As for Malora's other family members—her sister, uncle, nephew, and nieces—I haven't seen them around the house; perhaps they moved out during my absence.

MAY 20, 1903. The household has largely returned to normal. So far, we have had no signs that *La Limace* is seeking ingress anew, but it would be foolish of us to relax our guard. The beast will return.

Meanwhile, I am noticing a gradual but steady transformation in Malora. Daily, in disturbing ways, she is taking on the appearance of an altogether different being. Whereas she had always been quite short, she is now considerably taller. Her torso has become elongated, as have her arms and legs. Her fingers are thin and tapered. My wife's figure had always been petitely voluptuous—now it is excessively lean. Her once-rosy cheeks are now very pale—a ghastly white with an increasingly bluish cast.

67

And, strangest of all, her head has changed its very shape. It is growing narrower and longer, the chin somewhat pointed. Her hair is even changing color. The raven black locks I once loved now resemble tufts of sallow corn silk. Seated quite still in her leather-upholstered chair, the velvet curtains drawn to block the afternoon sun, she stares at me with drab, sunken eyes, and says nothing.

Concurrent with this change process, a semi-transparent sheath of fine gauze-like material is spreading over her entire body—some kind of cocoon-like encasing structure draping itself over her features, which remain visible through it. Could this be the so-called "shroud" of which the occult lecturer de Atal spoke, its development triggered by the forceful separation of Malora from the vile *Limace?*

I wonder if she understands what she is becoming? For it becomes clearer with every passing day that Malora is developing into the same type of being that Azrael has been for centuries. One of the more preposterous claims that Henri de Atal had made in his lecture comes back to haunt me: that after many years of being under the parasitic control of *La Limace*, the human host ultimately enters a new stage of existence in which their body is greatly transformed, and they become, in effect, a radically different type of creature physically and spiritually. The most notable sign that this change has begun is the formation of a cocoon-like growth of tissue called the "shroud"—initially around the small of the victim's back where the mollusk's gigantic appendage penetrates the torso. Eventually, the shroud spreads in all directions until the person's body is completely enclosed within its diaphanous fibers. Inside that cocoon, largely unobserved by other humans, the victim's body undergoes numerous severe alterations, after which, the nascent organism bursts forth, reborn in new flesh, frees itself from the domineering mollusk (or in this case, from the attentions of her loving family), and begins its new existence. The fully formed adult creature not only separates itself from *La Limace* but strives to counteract the evil that the mollusk perpetrates in the human realm, seeking out the fiend's intended victims and—to the extent possible—protecting them from its insidious attacks.

If this is what is actually happening to Malora—and there is every indication that it is—then she will be like Azrael: a partly mortal, partly supernatural crossbreed, radiantly angelic when the occasion calls for it, yet undeniably ghoulish in other ways. She will stink of the grave, yet men will weep tenderly when they lay eyes upon her unearthly beauty. Sadly, Malora will no longer be mine alone, and will cease to act as my wife, but will be freer than the saints in their hallowed tombs. I cannot imagine what mysteries the future holds for her.

Part 2

The King in Yellow

CHAMBER OF SHARDS

"He closes his eyes and a thousand cities ignite."
—old saying recorded in *The Tablets of Nhing*

Backlit by the rose pane,
The High Priest stands with
arms outspread, as if
to gather back the
fleeting rays of dusk.

Solitary in the Chamber of Shards,
the favored one holds a delicate finger
to her perfect lips and sucks
away a drop of blood.

Later, he will come to her,
in the fury of his long-pent lust,
but for an hour of dying light
she must lonely bide her time.

Her frivolous companions gather
at the end of a crumbling pier
extended over dark water,
tittering amid more somber speculations
of hues rumored to survive.

With each tick of the clock
he ponders the ineffable beauty
of his hoard of shattered windows.

A paradox of the sublime:
that which by law he owns
he is never truly at
liberty to possess.

For each variant shade of glass,
an army perished. With each
languid breath she exhales, a
part of him dies anew.

As the solar disk
sinks in the West,
luminous riches fade
to blackness and terror.

None see the love nor cruelty
in his shrouded eyes.
He feels their curious stares
and gasps in glory and sorrow.

In Her Hibernal Aspect

On that sultry summer night when no breeze stirred and the memory of midday sun still burned through my sleepless consciousness, I had foreseen this day, had known that my travels would take me to this desolate plain, had envisioned myself standing knee-deep in sere grasses, awaiting her arrival. We had conspired that night; I had promised her three souls would she but spare my own, and now I was making good on my word. I recognized the appointed place by the multitude of wind-worn tombstones scattered about, their blighted faces staring up to the emptiness of heaven.

"Don't bother trying to read the names thereon inscribed," she had advised me. "Time hath stolen their identities. Those are the expired legions who precede us—lives not dignified by memory."

She had described just such a valley as this, its only feature being the surrounding piles of mutely colored rocks. Yes, this was the chosen place, but where was she? Did she remember our assignation? I was to come when the autumn turned cold, when life drained from the land and the days grew indistinguishable in their uniform gray bleakness.

"You will know it is time when summer seems hopelessly remote, when you finally despair of escaping the long and brutal winter ahead. Then come to that place in haste, and we will complete this sordid business. You will give me what I desire, and I will set you free—for a while, anyway."

I had done exactly as she instructed, having little choice in the matter. For one in such an exalted position, I had very little real power. The three women I was prepared to surrender had given me much pleasure—there was no question of my having enjoyed their company—but I had no other option in the long run than to sacrifice them to save myself. Their presence at court had been tolerated for a season, but that season had ended, and now the ties must be severed. I wished them no ill, but they were expendable, being lost street-girls, interchangeable and easily replaced when summer returned and the festival began anew.

Was I mistaken in believing her promise to be sincere? I did not think so, yet I had to wonder, for there was no one there to greet me, no voice calling out my name—only the harmony of yellow grasses joining in the empty song of wind.

I turned to face the direction from whence I had journeyed and was about to retrace my steps homeward, when from out of the storm-clouded east a form came rushing toward me with great speed: a wild, fluttering apparition. This shape bore no physical resemblance to the voluptuous being I had encountered in the hillside vault last summer, the one they call *Sweet Childe of Chaos,* yet by its malign spiritual essence, I knew it to be that same entity in her hibernal aspect. Entirely cloaked in flowing black silk robes, her diaphanous scarves—like innumerable rippling limbs— undulated about her, although there was not enough force in the wind to accomplish such a thing. Before I could make sense of what I was seeing, she was upon me, one black-gloved hand extended, a finger raised in question. Her words echoed as if she were still lodged in her mountain cavern, entombed in cold rock.

"You mean to keep your promise, priest?" she asked.

"I do."

"But you arrive alone. How is that?"

"No, I did not bring them with me. That is true. But I will release them unto you, as agreed. I saw no need in them accompanying me on this journey—a showy escort of hussies, thereby encouraging further gossip. I will tell you where to find them and, if I am not greatly mistaken, you will have no trouble in securing these exquisite souls."

"Indeed. I may take them there, as well as here, with your leave. Where are they?"

"Back in the city, at a crumbling ruin of a structure built out over the lake on stilts. This edifice houses my collection of stained-glass windows salvaged from the demolished ancient homes of the great metropolis. It is a place to which I often repair for hours of silent meditation. It is also where I have frolicked with these Cyprians. When I am in the mood for their tender company, I send word for them to meet me there, as I have done this day. When the weather is fine, many are about to witness their comings and goings, but now that the lake is frozen, none will have seen their arrival, and none will notice that they never leave the hall. You may find them lingering there and take them by my invitation."

She said nothing in reply. I knew the arrangement was acceptable by her sudden departure. The only sound was a sharp inhalation caused by the inrush of air filling the vacuum in the space she had lately occupied, followed by the gentle sighing of redistributed vapor. I departed myself, knowing the matter resolved, and that the chamber of my repose would be peacefully vacant when I returned to the city—as I like it when I have need of reflection.

PROCESSION OF THE EXPENDABLE

The King's attendants on his garden isle
Thrash fey palm fronds to cool the royal brow,
While others dance unchaste to raise a smile;
They hope to please their fickle King somehow.
Beloved most are those who twirl at dusk,
Beguiling him with spinning forms sublime,
Their sable locks exuding scents of musk;
Embody they the spirit of this clime.

All pray he'll choose them from among the throng
And raise her status to a queen's, or more,
If only while the moon shines on the hill.
They don't expect to know his passion long
Beyond the time that he'd allot a whore;
Their souls discarded once he's had his fill.

The Dying King

As King of Carcosa and High Priest of the Children of Folly, this Yellow One wields great power, and yet there are Those who have dominion over Him, and Others who bear dominion over Them, for behind all Things are Other Things, unseen but felt, in profusion unto Infinity.
  —Marginalia in an ancient copy of *The Tablets of Nhing*

The King stood at the tower window, his eyes narrowed to mere slits, and gazed out over the frigid valley below. Dead forests, withered pastures, ruined estates, derelict towns, untrodden roads, sere rivers, dry lakes—all of it his, an embarrassment of gloomy riches, shrouded in dirty snow. And yet he felt utterly impoverished, as penniless as any beggar. For despite his vast wealth as recorded on countless sheaths of parchment, there was not one thing in this miserable realm that he could really hold on to, that he would possess in a year's time, or even in one cycle of the Moon. For the King was dying—that was the raw truth of it. His personal physician had revealed this sad fact an hour ago, and for his honesty the man had been beheaded. Nothing fair about that, but while Death cannot be punished, her messenger can be. As the man's still-warm body twitched on the stone slabs of the courtyard and the drunken executioner wiped

79

a copious smear from his blade, the King called for his wife to be escorted—or dragged—from the chamber of her seclusion to an audience with her lord and master.

While he awaited the Queen, the King dispatched his generals, for an old score needed to be settled. Evidence of his undiminished wrath would be visible within the hour—smoke billowing on the horizon where the betrayers dwelt. She soon arrived, preceded by her belligerent protestations echoing through the halls.

"You know I am done having congress with you," she complained, not attempting to conceal her boredom with this disruption of her afternoon. "In keeping with the law, I have surrendered my connubial obligations to the clutch of clucking whores now adorning your private quarters. Why trouble me at this late date in our much-storied history?"

"I am aware of the situation, dear wife, and of our current legal arrangement. And believe me, I would not trouble you for amorous favors even were you willing, as once was the case, so many years ago. That ship, as they say, has sailed … over the world's edge and into the fiery pits of Hell, for all I care. My whores serve me quite well, thank you. Better than you ever did. I have no complaint on that score."

Insulted, the Queen's eyes widened and her nostrils (from which a single wispy white hair protruded) flared, but she held her tongue and allowed him to proceed.

"No, I summon you here not to ask for a comfort that you have no inclination to give. I'm not a fool, and I still have my pride, despite your continuous efforts to relieve me of that burden. My purpose is simply to inform you of the fact that I am dying. A foul adversary has set her teeth deep into my being, and I am no match for her in either ferocity nor endurance. In a fortnight, perhaps sooner, I will take to my bed—alone—never to rise again. And a day or two after that, you will be free of me—a grace for which you have long bided. This is my final gift to you, although I have no say in the giving. The only thing I ask in return is that you allow a respectable amount of time to pass before you dispose of my personal effects and obliterate all trace of my legacy. Go through the motions of mourning until spring, if you would be so kind. Black always was becoming on you."

Her demeanor quickly changed from one of weary indignation to rapt attention. The hint of a smile flickered at the corner of her mouth.

"I hear no objections, wife, no entreaty that I defy the Dark Angel and linger indefinitely by your side on the throne, if not in the royal bed."

"Nor shall you."

"As expected."

"I promise you the public display of my bereavement will not be abbreviated, my lord. You have my word on that."

"Excellent. Then I'll bid you farewell, my queen, until we meet again in some future incarnation."

"I am certain you won't allow that to transpire!"

He laughed. "No, actually I won't. I'll make sure we don't encounter one another again, in any realm, under any stars. But it seemed the decorous thing to say to a queen."

"As it is. Are we done here, your highness?"

"We are finished."

She curtsied and left, escorted by the same guards who had brought her. He detected a new jauntiness in the Queen's step that shaved ten years off her age.

*

The sun had set a quarter-hour ago, and still he was staring at the red band of ebbing light clinging to the hills.

"It diminishes like sand passing through the neck of an hourglass, grain by grain, until it is all run out."

"Of what do you speak, my lord?"

81

Hers was a gentle, youthful voice, full of warmth and grace. The comely young woman stood close behind him, her small hand rubbing his back just above his shoulder blade. He knew the tenderness he sensed from her was real. That she was paid to be there was an accident of economics. He just as likely could have met her at Court, were she the legitimate daughter of a nobleman, but she was the bastard brat of a cobbler, and his first view of her voluptuous charms had been when she stepped out of her filthy rags and he saw that her natural beauty had not been mitigated by the difficulties of being raised in poverty.

"I speak only of time, and of life. Or of the day's light—take your pick."

"You are too serious, my lord. Come to bed and I will give you good cheer, and fire against this chilly eve."

"We kings are called to high seriousness, child. It's what we do best."

She took his hand, tugging lightly, and he followed her into the darkened chamber where a single candle flickered at the bedside.

She was one of a thousand such splendid beings who had passed through his life. In the eyes of the law, he owned each one of these lovely creatures, fully, in body and soul, but he knew that was an empty advantage. Own them as he may, he could not hold onto them beyond an hour or a day, or however many fleeting moments he had remaining. They entered his life, and they left it. After he was gone, they would serve other masters, and love other men. Assuredly, he could prevent a succession of his rights by having them slain, but he had no wish to harm these lost children. Life would bring them enough pain; why should he add to their store of that coin? This one was especially kind. He hoped she would remember him with affection afterward. In the morning he would send her away with the rest of the Cyprians, each maid's purse ponderous with gold, to secret locations where his vindictive Queen would never find them.

*

Death appeared in his chamber on the third night after he had taken to bed in the throes of a fever. He had expected her countenance to be foul and grotesque, and for her person to reek of the charnel house.

"Don't be ridiculous," she said in a voice as tender as that of any of his sullied maidens. "I am the instrument and agent of your passing, not a victim of mortality myself."

She reached out her hand, and he saw that it was fair.

"I am too weak, Mistress. I cannot lift myself up. I cannot go where you lead."

"Then I will join you in your bed, my Tattered One, and take you where you lie."

She lay down beside him, aglow in her radiance, and he was comforted.

"Even this will not last," he uttered feebly, a smile on his parched lips.

"It will not. But you shall have other days, and other queens, my beloved. Nothing stays lost forever. The wind blows and the sands drift, but what has been before will be again. There is no ending, only gatherings and dispersals. Trust me; I will spirit you away."

"Do I have a choice?" he asked with what little strength he had left.

"Not really. You know better than that."

"Then I will trust you, as I must."

To his relief, he found her the kindest and gentlest lover of them all, and he had no regret.

Caressa's Song

Betimes he doth consume these flowers,
knowing they shall bloom another day.
—The Tablets of Nhing

1.

One cold and foggy morning
the King beside the lake
met the fair Caressa,
her chastity to take.

He bid her to escort him,
concealing what he planned.
"Carcosa now awaits us."
He offered her his hand.

Demure, the maiden followed,
submitting to his lust.
She gave her virtue hallowed—
her heart knew only trust.

"Forever thee I'll love," she sighed,
He called his guards; anon she died.

2.

Next spring the lake was thawed,
surrendering its dead,
and left upon the shore—
a corpse with yellow head.

The necrosed lass arose,
on withered limbs she strode
straight through a haunted wood
toward the King's abode.

By stealth of dark she gained
the Monarch's feathered bed
and she lay down, a ghoulish bride,
as if they had been wed.

"Forever me you'll love," she sighed,
and terror-struck, he swiftly died.

The Cyprian's Tale

For the Yellow One hath entered into a bond with the Sweet Child; that he will deliver unto her a sacrifice of that which is precious in his sight, in the consideration of which she shall allow him to persist another season.

—unattributed annotation in a spurious copy of *The Tablets of Nhing*

I was newly arrived in the city and woefully ignorant of the cruel ways of its inhabitants, being a simple girl from the provinces: unschooled except by my own dear mother, of humble birth, and given to flights of foolishness. Bringing only a purse half-full of lowly copper coins that too quickly were exhausted, by my third day I felt the bitter anguish of hunger and involuntarily joined the city's army of destitute wanderers, being turned out of the boarding house at which I had stayed for lack of means to pay rent. Thus, I spent many a restless night in haystacks and alleys, my virtue in constant peril of predation by a number of dishonorable men who happened to stumble upon my place of repose in their riotous and drunken meanderings.

This intolerable situation persisted for too long, until, by some great stroke of fortune, I met a kind girl who took pity upon my plight and advised me to cleanse my face and habiliments as best I could and relocate myself to a certain public square where, that afternoon, officers of the Court would select from among the Cyprians assembled a few girls to entertain the King, be they young, of pleasing countenance, and not sullied by rough life in the streets.

"But I am no whore!" I protested, despite the pangs in my belly that argued otherwise, as well as the crying out of my soul for sanctuary that bid me to acknowledge my state of need and make whatever concessions were necessary to alleviate this present hardship. "I do not sell myself to men for money. You have judged me quite wrong, dear sister, although I cannot blame you, given my current aspect. I do not look a proper lady, I grant."

"Nay, my innocent one—we are all whores in this Man's world. It's merely a matter of time before you accept the terms of the deal. Want will decide your fate, not virtue nor principle."

Knowing she spoke truth, I thanked her and gained directions to the square, which was very near to the palace, it turned out, at the very heart of Carcosa. There, after much jostling and elbowing, I found myself well positioned among the teeming harlots who crowded the place at the appointed hour. The King's men promptly arrived and forthwith ran off all the aged, diseased, uncomely, toothless, lame, and odoriferous competitors; I was not surprised to survive this initial thinning of the ranks. The men then grouped the remaining ladies by means of assessing their beauty and freshness, and although I was not the first girl chosen to join the preferred lot, I did make that second sorting, and thereby was among the few fortunate lasses who were escorted to the palace that day.

Thus, my circumstance changed from one of stark privation to a life of opulent luxury. We were gently stripped by demure maidens, our foul rags burned, and the ashes scattered by the soothing winds that eternally played about the parapets. Bathed in warm pools whose waters were fragrant with exotic herbs, our voluptuous forms dried by the languid rays of sunlight, fragrant rare oils rubbed onto our immaculate skins, our tresses brushed to a silky sheen and our pretty faces adorned with precious cosmetics, we were veritable visions of loveliness, one and all.

Rendered thus suitable for a King's company, we patiently awaited him, squandering many an hour on idle gossip, wanton laughter, and the playing of frivolous games. And although we thought he would never appear, as the days turned into weeks and the weeks accrued into months, arrive he did late one fine day, escorted by his ancient Queen, some favored members of the court, an entourage of hangers-on, and various minstrels and fools.

We had heard rumors of his legendary charisma and power, and although he was visibly of an advanced age, to a degree unknown among common men, at the same time it was true that he exuded an aura of unsurpassed strength and undeniable physical charm, which every woman among us immediately found irresistible, although he was old enough to have sired their father's father. I, too, was subject to his allure, despite my keen wish to remain as chaste as the day I had left my home. He was garbed in the tatters of a long priestly robe—not ruined by the ravages of many years' service but shredded by design—and the greater part of his physiognomy was shrouded from our sight by a fine silk scarf of yellow hue that was wrapped snugly about his head, so that only his eyes were exposed to our curious gaze. Ah, but what stabbing black orbs they were! And how they pierced my heart and penetrated my soul.

"That's why they call him the King in Yellow," whispered one of the girls most ill-advisedly. "Because of that filthy piss-colored rag covering his face, and what a horror it must be, that he hides it so." We shushed her, but too late, for the guards had overheard, and two of them rushed forward, seizing the impertinent tart by her arms and dragging her screaming to the high walk's edge where they tossed her over the side, and she fell to her death.

None of us dared gasp in repulsion but pretended we did not see this act of murder, and all continued to smile upon the King with real or feigned desire that he would choose her for his evening's entertainment.

"Well, there's one less whore you'll catch the clap from," sneered the Queen.

"Shut thy foul trap, old woman," he replied, snorting with mirth at her jibe.

He thoughtfully rubbed his chin through the scarf as he examined each girl displaying her charms, and then resumed speaking, this time addressing his entourage and not his wife. "Three delightful mistresses I have at present to warm my bed. One more I require, for a fourth has gone off to her confinement, being with child...."

"You had her killed when you learned of the pregnancy," interjected the Queen.

"Departed, I say, to a convent where she will bear my bastard while attended by the finest midwives in the land."

"Her bloated corpse washed up on the shores of Lake Hali yesterday morning, they say, but who am I to judge?"

"Indeed—just who are you, woman? A Queen in name only, not in function, for the honey has seeped from the comb, and the bees have abandoned the hive."

With that insult, the Queen huffed indignantly and stormed off, lifting her hem so she wouldn't trip, and leaving the King unmolested to select the missing girl's replacement—who was I, most unexpectedly—from among the young women presented for his approval. At that joyous moment, the minstrels broke into song, the fools began to juggle, the hangers-on lewdly cheered, and I was removed to a secluded chamber where I joined the other royal mistresses preparing to serve his pleasure.

That evening, moments after sunset, the King did come to us, speaking much foolishness, his tongue made loose by wine, and we lay beside him on divans and dallied such as lovers do, each sporting with him in turn, but none of this frolic resulted in him knowing us carnally as men do know their wives, for he wished for the ultimate intimacy to occur in a more private setting, one that bore a special significance to him. This place, I learned from the others after he had left us, was on the docks, in a derelict structure that housed the collection of art objects, stained glass and war trophies he had gathered over the years. He called it his "Chamber of Colors," and it was known only to his closest confidants and a few trusted servitors. We were to go there secretly on foot, at midnight, when all the household was asleep except the Night Watch, and he would meet us there and make good his promises of Love.

Desiring still to keep myself pure against all odds, I yearned to flee the palace, to leave the city entirely, but dared not disobey the King's desire that we join him later, out of fear that he would have me killed as he had so many others before, and so I accompanied my sisters when the hour came, the four of us running barefoot from the palace to within a hundred steps of the docks. There, within sight of his cherished Chamber, I stumbled and took an awful spill in the dirt, twisting my ankle. The others did not stop to help me up, nor even to make sure that I was not badly harmed. They were most fearful of being tardy and thereby displeasing our King, and so I was left behind, on the dark road, my gown soiled from the fall I had suffered, nursing a swollen ankle. At length, although in great pain, I found I was able to stand and then limp toward the dock, ever watching the motley lit windows of the warehouse wherein my sisters awaited the King's arrival.

The decaying edifice on stilts over the dark water was a sprawling structure of many compartments, any one of which might hold my sisters. As I approached the nearest window and peered inside to see if I could find them before the King made his arrival, some uncanny movement in the sky caught my attention.

91

Looking up toward the Moon's ivory face, I saw a wondrous black shape flitting through the air, fluttering like a wind-blown banner on a field of battle, but having no resident color beyond the empty ebony shade of the celestial deep. It soon grew closer and of larger aspect and fell upright to the Earth without a sound and took on a familiar shape: that of a most handsome woman, but clearly, she was no ordinary lady. This remarkable creature in black silk robes was one that I recognized, although I had never met her, for it was the supernatural person known as the Sweet Childe of Chaos: she who holds dominion over the King in Yellow, for it is said that all Lords have an Overlord, and for every Power, there is yet a Higher Power. This I knew because it was told in the ancient books my mother read to me as a lass, that I might not be ignorant, though poor.

That which transpired next I was not prepared to witness. The Sweet Child—not the King, who was woefully absent, and had no intent to appear—entered the chamber and sought out the three Cyprians who by now had wandered into my view, although they did not in turn observe me. And she did utter in a voice as cold as Winter's blast, "I hereby claim that which he has promised me," unto the girls, who were mightily puzzled and showed great fear in their countenances, and then she did tear them completely asunder, making horrid messes of their flesh, and leaving the pale walls and floors of the King's favorite chamber besmirched with blood. Turning quite slowly, she looked me in the eye, and said "Only three souls was the promise as made. You are free to go, young miss—this time," and with that she flew off suddenly, as witches are wont to do.

That night I fled the city, and never returned. Although I was long in the grip of a terrible dread, none of the King's men ever came looking for me, for I do not believe the King had troubled to know my name, nor whence I had come. Nor did he seem to care that I had escaped his grasp, for there are many Cyprians in

Carcosa, and I was but one of them, expendable to him whether I be living or eternally at rest.

The Hour of Transference

I t is the hour of transference, the melancholy lingering of daylight that falls between the graceful setting of grainy Aldebaran and the fiery plunge of the Hyades below the crest of volcanic rock that rims the city of Yntill, as I stand motionless on the precipice, facing west, a warm breeze fluttering the folds of my tattered robe, gazing with yearning eyes into the lurid azure penumbra that marks the unseen shifting of vaster dimensions. Verily, I am lost in poignant memories, having witnessed the innumerable transformations that transpire over the course of infinite cosmic cycles, and thus know to hold my tongue and bide my time, resolutely ignoring the calls of these impatient celebrants, Camilla and her wanton sisters, attempting to lure me into their debaucheries, erroneously assuming that all-commanding means will grant illimitable license; nay, I abstain, for I have learned the wisdom of a strictly maintained decorum, and I know the supernal strength that comes from never succumbing to carnal weakness nor yielding to the transient temptations of the flesh which always result in dishonor, and I stand my ground, ignore their strident, seductive pleas until they fall away, drifting off one by one to leave me alone with this splendor of diminishing illumination. And when the final moment arrives, and the region of Demhe is cast into blackness with only the jewel-like stars lighting the vaults of heaven, I know the stranger will step forward out of the ebon shadows—as he always does—bearing before him the sigil of Truth, and he will allow to fall from his terrible face the Pallid Mask so that all may see the seething plethora of maggots roiling in putrescence that is his noble physiognomy. Then, at last, comes the shrieking of the Winged Beasts, and the city will be awash in crimson rivulets of hot, healing blood.

PART 3

TOMBS & OTHER LOVECRAFTIAN HORRORS

THE CRAWLING DEAD

When I was a child, my Aunt Renee was murdered. She was beaten to death with ball-peen hammers by men who were attempting to extort money from her. This was in the 1950s.

I should explain that she owned a small antique shop in a run-down part of downtown Los Angeles. It was in a crumbling brick building. Whenever my parents and I visited Aunt Renee, we parked in the alley and entered the dank, poorly lit, narrow shop from the back. This entrance led us through a jumbled storeroom piled high with yellowed newspapers and past a small, dirty bathroom with a toilet that never stopped running and a perpetually burnt-out light bulb that hung from a chain.

The shop was always as still as a tomb ... a shrine for old glass and knickknacks, for darkly polished wood carvings and other relics of the past. What with the accumulated dust and city grime on the windows, daylight never fully penetrated into the building's recesses. There were seldom any customers.

She was killed there, in the shop. We were later told that hoods had come around to Aunt Renee many times, demanding that she pay them protection money, and each time, she had stubbornly refused.

Apparently, they had lost patience with her ... or, perhaps they sought to make an example of her for the surrounding businesses. At any rate, my father received the grim news in a phone call from the police one Saturday morning. We drove up to her home in a quiet old residential neighborhood in L.A. I can't recall the exact area. The houses were fairly old—dating from about 1900 to 1920—but not dilapidated. There were a number of better-make automobiles parked on the street; a glossy black Packard sedan that might have been my aunt's stands out in memory.

An atmosphere of funereal gloom pervaded the home of my newly murdered aunt. Not knowing what to expect next, I sat waiting on the sofa in the living room—which was unnaturally darkened by the drawn curtains—while in the kitchen my parents spoke in hushed tones with my aunt's younger sister, Elizabeth.

It had always been clear to me that Renee was the strong one, the domineering older sister, while Liz played the role of the cowering and whimpering dependent little sister. To the unclouded vision of a child, it was obvious that Liz lived in the shadow of Renee. Now that Renee was dead, what would Liz do? Liz seemed incapable of living her own life. That the world would consume her whole, I had little doubt.

I ate candies from the dish Aunt Renee always placed out on the coffee table for company—chocolate disks speckled with tiny white candy beads. *Nonpareils,* I believe they're called. From the kitchen came Liz's moans and sobs. I tried to force myself to imagine what Aunt Renee had looked like when the police found her with her skull crushed and her face beaten to a pulp by hammers, but I was unable to conjure up any image more vivid than a general impression of obscene gore. I could not fathom the spiritual darkness of men capable of such brutality ... could not comprehend how human hearts could be so cruel.

Now, Aunt Renee's house was big and sad and empty without her. I wondered: did her essence linger in the shadowed hallways and cling to the dusty lace curtains and graying doilies?

Aunt Renee had always appeared incredibly old to me. She was perhaps eighty at the time of her death, and I could not remember a time when she wasn't stooped over, her back rudely hunched with arthritis, her chin drawn as long as a witch's and her face deeply channeled with wrinkles. But perhaps her most elderly characteristic had been her voice: a weird, high-pitched squawk that grated like fingernails on a chalkboard, dry and ancient and Old Worldly.

I pictured her stiff and lifeless corpse, prone, still hump-backed even in death, the face battered beyond recognition by the round, cold steel hammer-heads. I pictured those sinister men who had killed her and felt unease gnawing at my stomach. There would have been glass art objects shattered on the shop floor around her ... the entire shop contents trashed ... blood smears everywhere. And some substance that could only be her violated brains.

I was not close to my aunt Renee, and therefore I was not so much saddened as terrified by her death. The stark fact of a gruesome murder being committed against a near relative haunted me for years. For long after, I had trouble sleeping, and a general sense of apprehensiveness—the gut knowledge that terrible things could and might happen to anyone, and that none of us were ever truly safe from potential violence—has never left me. Eventually, the immediate horror of her murder faded, to be replaced by other fear-inspiring events. Later it was the Kennedy assassination ... the Watts riots ... the Tate-LaBianca murders. I developed a sixth sense that somehow allowed me to perceive the growing chaos that sprawled out there on the fringes of our civilized society. And where others perhaps saw only the hushed city skyline at dusk, I saw imminent madness and horror soon to descend upon the coldly lit streets of district after district, receding into the formless night.

101

As far as I know, Aunt Renee's killers were never caught. No doubt they went on to commit other atrocities, never stopping to think of the effect their wanton sprees might have had on the sensibilities of an impressionable young boy, forever shattering his false sense of security.

Now I have to tell you about Aunt Renee and the mummies.

Not far from her house was a museum. I want to say it was the old L.A. County institution, but it couldn't have been, as I distinctly recall that this museum was set deep in a hillside adjoining Renee's property, and that it was entered via narrow, tunnel-like passageways with walls of damp-stained concrete or rock.

Besides, it seemed to be a museum of death.

Before her murder, we had often combined a visit to my Aunt's with a trip to this odd little neighborhood museum. Among the bizarre treasures on display was a room full of ancient mummies and preserved corpses. One from Pompeii—a twisted, blackened wretch frozen in gray lava and ash—always sickened me with revulsion at the strange realities of human disintegration.

The mummies and preserved bodies were on view in lighted display cases built into the walls. Their stiff and dried forms lay in eternal repose under the glow of a weak incandescent bulb. I liked studying them and would linger as long as my parents would permit, although it made them suspect morbid tendencies in their son.

Somehow, I had picked up the idea that these spaces behind the glass containing the mummies were interconnected by means of a network of tunnels. I even suspected other, outreaching tunnels that connected the spaces to the outside world of the living. And I thought that the corpses had reached their final resting places under their own power, by more or less crawling through these tunnels.

102

It seemed to me that if the dead could indeed move, they would hardly be capable of standing and walking. But crawling—long and hard and laborious—did seem a possibility.

After Aunt Renee died, we made one final visit to that macabre hillside museum. My parents went on ahead, leaving me behind to dally in the mummy room. I studied the Pompeii Horror—as I called it—then moved on to the Egyptian mummies and was about to catch up to my mom and dad when something made me go back to have a second look at the Pompeii Horror.

Next to it was a newly built case that showed signs of fresh carpentry. Sawdust littered the floor, and the trim had yet to be painted. It had been empty a moment before, a plain bed of dirt awaiting its occupant. Now, emerging into that new space, was Aunt Renee, wrapped cocoon-like in her old black dress, which had become ripped and dusted with the powdery soil of the tunnels. Her poor bashed head was a sad and gory mess. She was struggling through a small trap door on the side of the case. Beyond that door was the dirt floor of a tunnel leading off into an unthinkable darkness.

I was stunned … hardly able to believe my eyes. I blinked, but it was her, all right. The hunched back was unmistakable.

I watched in awe as she wriggled with tremendous effort into place, then gradually settled down into a rigid stillness befitting the dead. For long minutes I gaped at the appalling ruin that had been her head; it was far worse than I could have imagined. The need to help in some way kept me pressed against the cold glass, but there was nothing I or anyone could do for her now—she was beyond help.

So, I gave up, and went and found my parents, saying nothing to them of what I'd seen.

Like the murder of Aunt Renee, which remained unsolved, I never unraveled the mystery of that strange little hillside museum, and how Aunt Renee had come to join the mummies in their long wait for Kingdom Come. And this grotesque enigma, like the murder, has haunted me for all these years, as unsettling and as inexplicable as the very act of violence that brought her to that sad estate we call death.

In Nether Pits

A thousand steps
beneath the loam,
in nether pits
the ghouls call home,
I spied a face
I thought I knew,
a long-dead friend
all gone to grue.

Thus startled in
his native clime,
he fast withdrew
to shade and slime,
but not before
I thought I saw
a severed limb
grasped in his paw.

I thought to draw
him from the gloom
into the light
of that deep room
where hoary crypts
are stacked three deep
and subterranean
rivulets seep.

He would not quit
his hiding place,
would not reveal
his decayed face,
shrank from the torch's
lurid glow,
abhorred the truth
the light would show.

Memories fond of
days long past
compelled I save
this sad outcast,
or if he prove
beyond salvation,
dispatch him to
overdue damnation.

But as I crept
to where he lingered,
from all around my
coat was fingered,
then clutched, then ripped
by digits rotten—
a dozen hands
tore at the cotton.

Then I fast fled
that sunken room,
raced up the steps
and quit the tomb.
The ghoulish horde
were at my heels;
their arms reached out
like writhing eels.

A Visit to the Morelle
Family Tomb

nwisely I entered the necropolis at noon, abandoned the
searing glare of a febrile summer's day for the obsidian
gloom of its Stygian depths. Wandered I there amongst the
lower crypts like a man on a mission, and driven I was, for I sought
the noblest of crypts that fill chamber after chamber in the deeper
pits of that ancient hollow—the ancestral tomb of the Morelle
family, where the expired members of that distinguished clan enjoy
their eternal repose. What lured me there was an unwholesome
desire to visit the empty coffin wherein, someday, inexorably, my
cherished Lunulae—she of the golden Pre-Raphaelite curls and
lush velvet gowns—would lie forever immobile once Death had
laid claim to her animating spirit. The Alienists would call this the
soul of perversity, a morbid melancholia, but it was nothing that
dramatic; for I had merely resolved that if I could not be where
at that hour she lived and breathed and moved with the grace of
the black swans that glide upon the waters encircling her place
of seclusion, then I would relish the clammy, dust-laden air that
effused about her waiting sarcophagus. I would *now* be where she,
ultimately, would be *forevermore*. Oh, I knew too well the alienists'
complaint: I was playing a dangerous game by substituting
this pathological convenience for a vitality I was barred from

ever legitimately enjoying. Cared I nothing for their simpering objections; the thrill of the deed far outweighed any moral censure these mundane, unimaginative men might raise. With mounting anticipation, I passed by the remains of the countless throngs of my beloved's predecessors—their rows of marble effigies seeming to hail my bold endeavor—until I was stopped in my tracks by one shockingly familiar countenance. Aroused by my rude imposition, she was sitting upright in the plush casket reserved for my Lunulae: a woman strange yet known full well to me, bearing her likeness to a remarkable degree, yet all the more disturbing for that keen familiarity. For what I immediately observed was the ironic fact that all of the subtle characteristics that together had once comprised the living maiden's uncanny beauty were now transformed into foul markings of profane ugliness and depravity by force of the physical decay of her carnal being brought on by unrelenting mortality. Yes, this atrocity of female degeneracy bore an undeniable resemblance to the incomparable beauty I had loved and languished after, year upon year. And despite the extent of its decomposition, the infernal creature's form yet moved, a demonic energy illumining its eyes so as to pierce the darkness with their unholy stare. Fled I then from that accursed crypt, my frenzied heart pounding, unable to draw breath again until I had reached the safety of the surface and stood once more under a sky ruled by Reason. It was only much later that I learned of the cruel deception that had been played upon me; the beast I saw below was not my fair Lunulae at all, but the desiccated corpse of her long-deceased *mother,* from whom my beloved had inherited every aspect of her remarkable beauty. As for the cadaver's seeming aliveness—it was but a trick of my unhealthy state of mind, or so the alienists claim.

THE CRYPT OF NITOCRIS

Inspired by H. P. Lovecraft's "Imprisoned with the Pharaohs"

At Giza on the midnight sands,
I fell into fierce Bedouin hands.
A perilous drop by spooling rope
into a realm devoid of hope.

In chambers far below the Sphinx—
a woman's torso with head of lynx.
Of flesh, not marble, she was formed
in heaps of gore where beetles swarmed.

And hybrid mummies of King Khephren—
one half, hippopotami; the other half, men.
Parading through expansive rooms
more likely used as homes than tombs.

Then monstrous progeny, quite obscene,
foul issue of the ghoulish queen.
Offering praise with dusted breath,
to an Unknown God of Death.

Oh, countless wonders that blaspheme,
or was it all but fevered dream?

BLACK PANTHER

He traveled all day by foot, never once encountering anyone. His route took him through a wild region of dry, sparsely vegetated hills and arroyos filled with boulders. Scanning the horizon from each summit, he surveyed only further ranges and canyons. The abandoned mission was said to be sited in this country, although none had seen it for over a century. Rumors told of a crumbling ruin where once a noble structure had stood—a relic fallen prey to the depredations of relentless sun, encroaching nature, and the haunting spirits of its former occupants, the humble, hard-working fathers. Legend called it "The Lost Mission," for none knew its exact location, but some said the name actually implied "lost to the devil." Monsignor inspired fear among his flock; none dare oppose that fierce being. Some claimed a phantasmal beast, a giant cat of the hills, ever guarded the priestly wardrobe, lest some foolish thief purloin the Master's cloak.

Late in the day, the traveler found the antiquated edifice, its adobe walls yet erect but the ceiling decayed and in danger of collapse. The pews were all stripped out, pillaged by scavengers. With no candle to light his way, the interior was shroud in shadow and given over to spiders. Cobwebs hung in eerie drapery from the upper vaults. A coating of pigeon dung whitened the floor tiles. The air stank of age and decay. His treading raised motes that danced in the glow around gaping doors and windows. Exploring the depths, he surmised the looting had been complete.

Until, that is, he came upon the cabinet of antique liturgical vestments. These were untouched; superstition played a role in their survival. Removing them one by one, turning each robe this way and that to catch the rays of failing light, rich brocades and delicate embroideries were revealed. Silk and velvet shot with gold thread, these garments were fashioned from the discarded finery of courtly ladies, who made of their cast-off gowns gifts to clothe the monks. Each vesture more colorful than the last—reds, yellows, purples—he thought to take them all away, the lot too lovely for the rats and moths.

But then he came to that unholy relic: the green robe worn by the great Monsignor himself, the one some whispered was beholden to demons. Simpler in design than the others—for Monsignor pretended at humility—and heavily frayed from many years' use, the man's very essence clung to this vestment. This one garment the traveler folded with care, for it was precious—a terrible artifact from a powerful being. Closing the cabinet—the other items returned to their pegs—he made to leave, the bundle under his arm.

Just then, he spied two eyes across the dark chamber. Hot coals of fierce intent, glaring at him and the stolen relic. Stolen? From whom? The ghost of a long-dead padre? Or from the Church itself, a spiritual force even now in its sad ruination? The eyes demanded he restore the vestment to its place. They darted left and right. He imagined a ripple of satiny sinew, like wet tar against the night sky—a glistening ebony form, shifting in the darkness. Stalking him?

A raw terror such as he had never known seized his limbs, holding him, then releasing, and he bolted for the door, sure he would feel an overwhelming blow when that awesome predator pounced, ripping his flesh to crimson shreds. Certainly, the hammering of his heart would kill him, but it didn't, and with hot breath on his neck he burst from the mission and fled that unmapped site. Ran until his legs gave out, collapsing on a hillside, the bundle clutched to his heaving chest. The beast did not follow; he was free, or so he thought.

Walking most of the night, he escaped the accursed region. At dawn's glimmering, the traveler reached home. His heart swelled with greed, proud of this possession. But there was no joy in the owning. For on hot summer nights, when he awakens from fevered visions of a lost mission that no man has entered for over a century, he sees on the dark balcony two widely spaced eyes—accusing orbs, burning coals of eternal hate—the eyes of the panther.

ADMONISHMENTS FOR THE INCAUTIOUS

To spare thee horrific fright
when languishing souls
emerge from tree boles,
stay away from all windows at night.

So as not to provoke the undead,
do not venture deep down
into crypts below ground—
thou art better off snug in thy bed.

Yet fiends enter dreams without leave,
and cause massive alarm
as they inflict great harm:
interlopers who will lie and deceive.

A door that's locked four times is safe,
while bolted thrice is a curse,
and done sixfold is worse—
even numbers bar midnight's vile waif.

To be brave is no feat in the light,
yet when day has departed
even bold men stout-hearted
know spirits go marauding at night.

BENEATH THE VEIL

Awakening in a darkened chamber in a tangle of sweat-drenched bedclothes, his mind was empty of any shred of personal history or even disconnected traces of memory, except for two distinct episodes of recollected consciousness—those being separated by an interminable period of deep, dreamless sleep in the form of a profoundly blank oblivion. Given what seemed to him the obvious incompatibility of this enigmatic pair of memories, he suspected that one must be a purely physical event that had taken place in real life—something that had actually happened to him—while the other had to be either an hallucination or a dream, for given the conditions prevailing in either episode, the other one could not be true. But which was the dream, and which was reality? In what he suspected surely must be a highly bizarre situation, he really did not know. If the first of the two sets of mental impressions he held in his mind was based on fact, then life was very good; it was fully worth living. But if the second set of impressions proved to be the greater reality, then life was nothing less than unending horror, and he did not wish to continue living it.

The dreadfulness of the later possibility so terrorized him that for the present he could not find the inner strength to rise from the bed, and lay there motionless for what seemed like hours, reviewing the two sets of memories in as much detail as he had retained, hoping to discover a clue in either narrative that might reveal the true nature of one or the other.

The first memory—for their relative order in time was clearly fixed in his mind—took place in a modern-looking church in a small city. The quiet austerity of the building's décor led him to believe that it served some variety of Protestant assembly, although he could not determine the exact denomination. He was the groom at his own wedding, standing proudly on the chancel steps, nervously awaiting the imminent entrance of his young bride. Beside him stood his best man, the image of strength and confidence, with hands crossed gracefully before him, while seated throughout the church were his numerous friends and family, young and old, all of them happy to be sharing this life-changing occasion with him.

The organist began with a subdued prelude that seemed to go on for quite a while until finally, at the far end of the hall, the doors swung open and in came the flower girls carrying baskets overflowing with yellow blossoms. With an air of high seriousness, they marched up the aisle toward the altar. As they reached the chancel area and began to peel off alternately to the right or left and took their places on the steps, the organist suddenly launched into the wedding march, its deep bass notes resonating throughout the length of the nave, making the walls and floors vibrate. A moment later the bride and her father entered the church, arm in arm, and slowly proceeded up the center aisle, each step made in time with the slow, plodding beat of the music.

With delight-filled satisfaction the groom watched the guests all turn in unison upon the bride's appearance, captivated by her vitality and feminine allure on this, her wedding day. Members of the audience clapped softly at first sight of her, while some gasped audibly. He was a lucky man, indeed, to be joined together in holy matrimony with a girl of such innate charm, innocence, and goodness. He had chosen his bride well and looked forward to a lifetime of countless joys and blessings.

Following the bride and her father up the aisle were the bridesmaids who busied themselves with tending to her carefully coiffed hair, the gauzy white veil covering her face, and the train of her long white gown. The gown, sewn from the finest satin, shimmered in ways that displayed to great advantage a figure that was both as slender as a girl's and as voluptuous as a woman's.

After that, the time-honored steps of the ceremony passed by in rapid succession, with the arrival of the smiling cleric in his formal robes, the delivery of his sonorous incantations from an ancient book of sacred writings, the utterance of hallowed vows by the awestruck couple, and their solemn exchange of golden rings. All through these proceedings, the impatient groom yearned to see the bride's face without the impediment of the veil, for the translucent nature of its fabric and the fact that a strong ray of amber light was shining directly on it from a nearby stained-glass window prevented him from seeing clearly through the material and confirming that underneath it lay the cherished physiognomy of his betrothed, and not the malign visage of some interloping creature of wickedness and shadow.

But why, he wondered as he lay there in the darkened chamber remembering what should have been a joyous moment, would he fear that some inhuman monstrosity had been substituted for his beloved? The perversity of such a thought was in strong disharmony with the joy of the occasion. And yet, that's what he had thought as he stared at the practically glowing veil—that he detected some semblance of a dark, hideous face below its fabric that spoke more of the grave than of the wedding bower, and at the same moment he thought that he detected from her direction a whiff of rotten stench when he should have been inhaling her delicious womanly scent.

Thankfully, these pernicious doubts were scattered to the four winds the very second the cleric pronounced them man

119

and wife, and the groom lifted his bride's veil and kissed her passionately on her honey-sweet, all too human lips.

Thereafter flowed the many delights large and small of a happy wedding party: inscribing their names in the huge, leather-clad register volume kept by the cleric in a private room behind the altar; warmly greeting the many guests in a receiving line at the back of the church; a sumptuous feast of rare meats, delicate wines and exotic fruits in the lantern-strewn tent set up behind the church; a lively band of musicians playing festive tunes; dancing by the adults while the children ran and played; the simple pleasures of talking and laughter and watching others from across the room; and the one moment that all the single girls waited for when the new bride threw her bouquet into the air behind her and some lucky young woman caught it with the unspoken promise that she would be the next one to be chosen as a wife.

At some point during that leisurely summer evening before the sun went down behind the hills, the two of them slipped out unnoticed and escaped to start their married life together.

As simple as that. That's how he recalled this first set of memories. It could easily be a real part of his waking life, aside from that disturbing idea he had entertained about what her face might look like, hidden beneath the veil—a thought that had almost ruined the ceremony for him. And if this first set of memories was the reality, then the second set of memories that followed it must only be a nightmare, and not something worse.

He recalled nothing of what transpired after they had left the church. A vast sea of dreamless sleep had engulfed and obliterated all memory of his wedding night. Did they make love, or did they simply collapse in each other's arms, too tired for sensual pleasures? He did not know. Now he lay awake in what might be their honeymoon suite, and she could return at any moment to rejoin him in their common bed. Surely, she would, if that first set of mental impressions had been reality.

He recalled the wedding in the church with a melancholy yearning that was so poignant it was almost repellent, and that odd combination of positive and negative emotions made him wonder if it were only a wistful dream of what might have been, and not a recollection of something that was real.

He could not judge nor even guess at the duration of the period of dreamless oblivion he had then experienced, after they fled the wedding party. He might have slept for an hour, or an infinity of epochs may have passed by. There was no way he could take measure of its length, nor sound the mysteries of its depths. All he knew was that it formed a total break from all that had come before it—the degree of forgetfulness it provided was complete and perfect, and for that he felt like a great mercy had been bestowed upon him.

The second memory, or set of impressions that occupied his mind, had as its setting the site of a ruined temple. He and a few others were gathered on an expanse of weathered stone slab under a drab gray sky. Through the action of long ages and the effects of earthquakes and volcanism, the slab had become tilted and sat at a pronounced angle, so that when he endeavored to cross it, he was unsteady on his feet and feared he might stumble and fall. As before, he was an apprehensive groom, but this time at what seemed to be an occult matrimonial ceremony, and this was no sanctified church—it was a pagan enclave in a vast region of chaotic destruction and desolation. No organ played; the only sound was the mournful sighing of the wind across broken stone surfaces.

He stood facing the ritual's observers, keenly searching their eyes for an explanation as to why they were witnesses to this blasphemous rite but could read nothing in their expressions. A raggedly attired urchin girl climbed up on the far edge of the slab and shuffled lethargically toward him, a cluster of wilted flowers drooping from her dirty hand. She was followed by another, then

121

several more beggarly children—the decadent flower girls of this obscene mockery of a wedding.

Then he saw *her*—shambling alone toward him without the escort of a father figure—his bride to be. She had clambered over the jagged edge of the stone slab, in the act creating a long rent in the stained gown that covered her body from neck to ankle. The hole exposed one shriveled breast with a blackened nipple and a patch of gaunt belly mottled with blue bruises. A bevy of filthy bridesmaids soon emerged from out of the shadows of the surrounding piles of rubble and fell to accompanying her, some of them picking fitfully at her tattered garment, while others pulled small twigs and pale worms from her straggly hair. One of these waifish harpies, half naked with emaciated limbs caked in dried mud, clawed eagerly at the bride's veil of sackcloth while chattering incoherently, but was not successful in yanking it away. Had she done so, he wondered, what would the exposed face have resembled? A sultry demon? A dusky angel?

Her head awkwardly slumped downward with the chin resting against her sunken bosom, spindly arms hanging limply at her sides, his betrothed fitfully shuffled forward one laborious step at a time, pausing after each movement so as to gather her strength. It was not the way a vibrant young woman carried herself. This could not be the woman he loved! She was a pale sham of a bride—a cadaverous substitute for the woman he yearned to marry.

She shuffled ever closer, one terrible step at a time, until she stood immediately before him, the veil over her unknown aspect only inches from his eyes. She lifted her head until her eyes—could he detect them—would have been level with his own, and he sensed that she was staring directly at him through the density of the soiled covering. A dusty exhalation made the veil puff out, and he smelled the stench of her breath, rich with vile nuances of decay and foulness.

He would have turned and fled the temple ruin, would have abandoned this desiccated hag, had it not been for the dissuading presence of the evil priest in flowing crimson robes who began to chant unholy verses from an ancient book that he held spread open before the couple. Fearing both priest and bride, the groom dumbly repeated the vows read to him, ignoring their import, knowing full well he would not abide by them, could not keep nor honor them. It was all a profane lie, the babbling of devils, and he blocked the words and what they might mean from his consciousness, waiting only for the ceremony to end so that he might still make his escape. This was followed by the sacral exchange of rings, in which he slid a dented and twisted golden band formed in the likeness of a coiled snake onto her withered finger, and she, with great exertion, placed a band of hammered silver onto his left hand. At that juncture, the priest commanded in a frenzied tone, "Embrace the pristine consort!" and only with a tremendous effort of will power was the groom able to lift the soiled veil and gaze upon her face.

What he saw came as no surprise, but the sight did shock and horrify him: hers was the face of a corpse, one long buried and lately exhumed. The skin was dried and yellowed, a parchment-like relic that had split in places, revealing brown stretches of underlying bone. The lips were largely gone, with only crumbling remnants of tissue remaining around her mouth to partly conceal the lengths of ivory-hued teeth. The nostrils were reduced to black crusted holes. All this and more, one might anticipate when viewing the face of a cadaver. What was wholly unforeseen was the unnaturally glowing crimson eyes whose intense stare penetrated deep into his mind and soul.

At this final outrage he ought to have been completely panicked and repulsed; however, he was not. For within him now began to stir a strange desire, a perverse carnal lust that not only defied all reason but actually seemed to be driven by the horrors

123

to which he was being exposed. It was sheer madness, but he craved an obscene physical union with the loathsome atrocity now lewdly pressing against him, wished to join her forever and eternally partake of the infinite corruption in which she reveled in the company of these lowly others, her begrimed followers.

That was the remarkable conclusion of the second set of memories. He could not imagine what might have followed the hideous climax to the ceremony. Immediately after staring upon the visage of his spurious bride, he was plunged into the blackest, emptiest space conceivable, as if he had ceased to live, had in fact never existed at all. Lying there in the darkened chamber, he wondered if perhaps he had died from mental shock at that instant, but if so, then how could he have later awakened? It was all unfathomable mystery.

One set of mental impressions must be a dream, and the other must be a reality. No, that was not entirely true. It was possible both were dreams, and for some reason his real life had come to be completely hidden from him. He supposed it was also remotely possible that both sets of impressions were real, but there was no way he could rationally reconcile the two if that were the case. Well, he would soon know the answer to this mystery, for he would rise from the bed, exit the chamber, and see what kind of a world awaited him outside this dark, neutral space.

But before that could happen, a slender shadow suddenly appeared in the chamber's open doorway. Silhouetted against the moonlight was a female figure garbed in a long, pale dress. She was his bride, and this, their wedding night—but from which memory? The figure remained motionless for several long seconds, and then it began to shamble torpidly toward him.

OUT OF ARKHAM HILLS

I.

Some parched thing disturbs these trees,
bucking Death's gravitic reins,
stirs, and trembles like a leaf
that's aroused by scented breeze
from Arkham's ancient cobbled lanes,
quivers, lifts, and crawls in grief,
rising from the cloying bane,
drags toward the unmarked sill,
a yellow gleaming window pane—
beacon bright below dark hills,
creeps so slowly none would say
it moves at all, and none delay
its fated arrival,
its unlikely survival.

II.

Dry and frail, mired in mud,
corpse of one unfairly slain,
dreaming long her earthly dreams,
drawing comfort from spilt blood,
finding solace in their pain,
taking balm from echoed screams
that resound in witches' dreams.

III.

Some parched thing in this wood stirs,
fights the oceanic pull
Death exerts upon her husk,
strains toward the Moon that lures
high above the hill, and full—
sterling orb emblazing dusk,
fragrant with a beldam's musk.

INNSMOUTH BATHERS

The Marsh daughters wade out into the surf that laps at the Innsmouth shore, strangely fashioned tiaras of whitish gold rising from their bloated heads, their round, bulging eyes lidless and incapable of blinking, as the wattled skin on their necks quivers in the rank wind blowing in from Devil Reef. These gawky bathers under a mocking yellow moon frolic lewdly in the phosphorescent foam, shamelessly displaying their scaly white bellies, cooing to the mariners assembled on the beach: "Come join us in the waves! Trade your melancholy mortality for our life of everlasting joy! Lie beside us in the ancestral palace beneath the sea, home of Father Dagon and Mother Hydra, whose many deep terraces and gardens shall conceal and protect you. What have ye to lose, O forlorn sailors? A briny bride awaits you each, free for thy taking!"

Thus each man falls to inevitable temptation; as if in a daze, he strides out into the waters, toward his chosen undulating girl— half woman, half frog-fish obscenity; and thus he disappears, sinking under the foam, while beyond in the distance looms the incendiary glow of that accursed rock pile. Soon, on a moonless night when these same sailors are spied furtively loping down the abandoned alleys of Innsmouth toward a former Masonic hall where congregate the members of an esoteric cult, it will be observed that the change is already upon them, their forms having

127

degenerated into that which is less than human, while the leer of aquatic madness shall radiate from their round, bulging eyes, shall shine from those cold, unblinking orbs. All this is known in advance by the Marsh daughters, for they have wed many a man in the century since they first took to the harbor, their pale, distended bellies gravid with the seed of the Deep Ones.

INNSMOUTH SHANTY

Briny devils from the sea
Think they own a piece of me.
At their bidding I will come
Flipping through the tide like chum,
Sinking in the ocean's chalice,
Slipping down to Dagon's palace.

[*Refrain:*] So rally, boys, at Innsmouth
To frolic 'neath the waves
And drink brown ale,
Then we'll set sail—*
We'll not be any man's slaves!

The sea, like wine, inebriates,
The salt-rich air intoxicates.
Hybrid fools of dire estate
Beneath the waves must congregate.
Moved by forces in the blood,
To wallow in the sea floor mud.

[*Refrain:*] So rally, boys, at Innsmouth [etc.]

Frog-fish maids from South Sea isles
Lure us with their wanton wiles.
How can mortal men resist
Once they have been mermaid-kissed?

129

Into the deep we swim to spawn
In this, our final liaison.

[*Refrain:*] So rally, boys, at Innsmouth [etc.]

Begetting offspring by the score;
Into our nets finned schools do pour.
Our wives and daughters are bedecked
In gold from galleys that were wrecked
Upon the shoals past Devil Reef
Where many a sailor came to grief.

[*Refrain:*] So rally, boys, at Innsmouth
To frolic 'neath the waves
And drink brown ale,
Then we'll set sail—
We'll not be any man's slaves!

*Note: a bawdy variant has the line "Chase fishy tail—" instead of "Then we'll set sail—."

WASHED UP

The beach town where I lived was known to be dangerous after dark, and it was not unusual for early joggers to find a blue-faced corpse rolling in the icy tide on desolate, foggy mornings.

Sometimes they were the hapless victims of muggings—men who had reveled too freely in the seedy waterfront bars and then made the mistake of flashing a bankroll, their foolhardiness catching up with them in one of the narrow, poorly lit alleys that, like psychic drains, emptied from the town into the sea. I'd sapped a few of them myself in the old days to make the rent when there was no publisher's check in my mailbox and the streets were too near and too real.

Or they might be unwanted lovers, receiving their gristly discharge in a bleak hotel room with dirt-streaked windows where screams were often heard by the jaded tenants but never responded to.

Or a missing child, its small, pathetic body discarded like so much trash once a forbidden longing had been satisfied by some monster of eternal night.

It might have been any of these, or some other variety of victim in this terrible community where violent crime was an all-too-common event, but it wasn't. For the thing they found bobbing in the surf that morning hadn't lived among normal men and women for quite some time.

That it had once been human, or partly so, was apparent from its general form—two arms and two legs, five digits (webbed) on each hand and foot, a thick, ill-defined neck, what I'd call a humanoid head, and a fairly normal-looking torso complete with small genitalia, male in this instance.

Something about the thick folds of skin where the neck joined the head suggested a gill-like breathing apparatus to some witnesses, but others, in retrospect, dismissed this as mere sensationalism or fantasy.

The thing had been found by workers reporting for the day shift at the Sea Guild Tuna cannery. Sea Guild was housed in a decrepit old sheet-metal structure that creaked and groaned atop rotting pilings down along the most unsavory portion of the waterfront. I'd worked there myself for one hellish summer in 1965, before I discovered that I could support myself by writing truly God-awful drivel for the pulp-fiction magazines. That was during my so-called "early period," of course, before I was discovered by Tommy Cox, the highbrow New York editor. Tommy set me up with the literaries, and instead of cranking out pulp trash, I cranked out something called Art. It was still garbage, but it enabled me to leave the cannery, and it kept beer and steaks in the fridge.

Rumor travels like wildfire on the docks, and within an hour there were several hundred gawkers gathered around the freezer in Wong's Fish Market, and more of them spilling out onto the streets, trying to see the thing. They had it on ice because they thought it was dead, and like anything else that washed up, it would start to stink before long if they didn't refrigerate it.

Photographs were taken of the workers with their "catch." You can still see one of these—an age-browned 8-by-10 glossy—tacked up over the bar in the Cap'n's Tap, a shabby little tavern not two blocks from here.

The thing itself is long gone. Nobody's seen it since that

night when I dragged it up into my room with the help of two drunken longshoremen who'd been hired to stand guard over it by Wong, owner of the market. I should explain that Wong had also paid the cannery workers who found the creature fifty dollars each for rights to the thing—money which they immediately squandered on ale and whores.

All that's left now to prove that the thing ever existed is that faded old photograph, and a rusted iron slave bracelet that had been hack-sawed from the creature's ankle. Wong still has the bracelet and refuses to part with it. He's shown it to me innumerable times over a bottle of port, and I'll be the first to admit that it's quite a prize. Men from every port in the world have examined that crudely forged ring of iron, and yet not one of them has been able to decipher the cryptic lettering, stamped in a recessed band around the artifact.

Rusty and Bill, the two longshoremen, thought me insane that night as we lifted the thing from its bed of crushed ice, wrapped it in towels, and lugged it out the back door of Wong's Market, down the half a block to my hotel, and up the back stairs to my room on the third floor.

"It's gonna stink like hell in here in about fifteen minutes," grunted Rusty.

"More like ten." said Bill.

"I can handle it."

"So, what the frigging hell do you want this dead fish guy in your room for, Hank? You wanna hump it or something?"

"No. I want to meditate in its presence."

"He wants to play with himself while he's daydreaming about mermaids," suggested Bill.

"Look," I said, dropping my end—the thing's feet—on the top step of the stairs. "I'm paying you guys good money to let me keep this in my room until dawn. Then we move it back before Wong shows up at 6 a.m., and he pays you more for watching it

133

all night. You make out like bandits, and nobody is hurt. What the hell does it matter why I want it in my room? Maybe I'm a sick bastard. Maybe I want to sing to it. Maybe I want it to sing to me. Perhaps it reminds me of my dear departed auntie. What difference does it make? Now clam up and help me lug this thing inside before somebody sees us and Wong has our asses thrown in jail."

That shut them up good.

We flopped it onto my old sofa, but it looked awkward as hell like that, so we moved it over to one of my two kitchen chairs and carefully propped it up in a sitting position. Then I ran Rusty and Bill out of there, grabbed a cold one from the icebox, popped the pull tab, and sat down in the other chair to have a good look at the unfortunate creature.

I sensed something sad about it, as if it had endured long, unbroken episodes of suffering and despair. I wondered about that iron ring Wong had cut from its ankle. There was a short segment of heavy chain attached to a thick loop welded to the side of it. This poor bastard had been a captive, a slave or prisoner of some kind, somewhere. I imagined maybe some secret government biological experiment carried out on a deserted Pacific island, and this monstrosity, one of the subjects, had escaped into the waves, swimming like mad, crazy with fear, hating its tormentors. I guess it was possible, but not too likely.

An alien survivor of a maritime UFO crash? Then why the chained ankle? No, that didn't make sense.

I remembered an old movie I'd seen on late-night TV, a low-budget black-and-white production, where this guy in a rubber suit runs around, attacking scientists on a boat. I stood up, walked all around the thing three times, hunting for zippers, Velcro snaps, stitching, safety pins—there was nothing. That blue-green stuff it was covered in was real flesh.

"All right … what's your story?" I muttered into my beer can.

The thing's mouth-slit opened just a fraction of an inch, and sea water trickled out and ran down its chin and neck. I detected eyeball movement under its closed lids. A certain tension animated the musculature.

"Tell me all about it. I have all night...."

The lids opened suddenly, and there was a dull glow of life in its eyes. The thing gazed around the room in apparent confusion.

"My place. Not exactly the Hilton, but the rent is paid. You want a brewsky?"

It didn't decline. I took that as a 'yes,' and fetched it a cold beer. The poor bastard couldn't manage the pull tab, what with those webbed fingers. I popped it open for him, even lifted it to his lips. Most of the beer ran right out of the sides of his mouth, but he managed to swallow some of it. I guess it was agreeable, as he raised the can for the next swig by himself. I sat down again.

"This town stinks," I said.

No comment from Fishface.

"Okay, we don't have to talk, if that's how you want it. We can just drink in silence."

Ten minutes went by without a word between us.

I began wondering why I'd brought him up here. How had I known he was still alive? Maybe it was those strange dreams I'd been having for weeks, about an unnamed island rising up out of the sea, and finding bas-relief tablets with images of a Phoenician Fish God carved on them, and lots of little minions gathered all around, worshiping the damned thing ... or maybe I was just bored, looking for a novel way to pass the lonely hours after midnight.

"You're not from around here, are you?" I asked.

It turned its head toward the open window. We could both see the dark stretches of ocean out there.

"Yeah, I understand that much. But why? Who kept you prisoner out there? And was it on an island, a ship, underwater— what?"

A tear rolled down one of the creature's cheeks. He didn't brush it away.

When he finally did speak, at about three a.m., after we'd each drained a six-pack, it was gibberish. Malarkey about some joker named Kathulhoo, from Rullyea. Poor demented sucker. He was hopelessly insane. I'd met his type before in the cheap bars along the waterfront. They all sang the same old song about this ancient marine god and his human followers, and some baloney about mating season, with all the girls swimming out and becoming pregnant after frolicking among the reefs with K and his boys.... I'd heard that stuff a million times and it was nonsense, through and through. A rummy's wet dream. I pitied the poor deluded fool. He would be better off on ice in Wong's backroom. There was no way he could make it out on the streets.

It was just as well that l heard Bill and Rusty at that moment, stomping up the stairs. We'd have this guy packed in ice again before he could even think "hangover."

He was still babbling on about what a mean bastard that Kathy was, etc., when Bill busted into the room. Rusty was right behind him.

None of us were prepared for the outburst from the Sea Thing. I thought I was dealing with a typical melancholy drunk, but suddenly we had a mean and very active one on our hands.

He smashed my red kitchen chair into toothpicks. I threw the other chair, the blue one, at him, and he smashed it, too.

"No," I said sarcastically, holding up a hand, "please don't apologize. They're junk. Don't give it a second thought."

He bellowed out a wild, bestial cry of mortal agony.

"Nobody here's going to give you any argument on that score, Flipper...."

His last glaring stare at me was more one of terror than of hatred. I think he realized that I wasn't the enemy, although I wasn't much of a friend, either.

136

He was out the door and down the stairs before we could even say goodbye. We scrambled after him, but he was too fast for us and disappeared down an alley toward the beach. Following his tracks across the sand, we could see they ran straight into the pounding surf.

Rusty panicked. "We have to catch him, Hank! Wong will kill us when he finds out about this!"

"I can borrow a boat from Sammy," added Bill.

"Aw, what the hell. Let the poor bastard go. Maybe there's something out there that beats anything here. I'll deal with Wong; I'll tell him I put you up to it. He won't do anything. He knows I have friends. Hell, I'm a celebrity: 'the poet of the docks.'"

Wong wasn't too happy about losing his prize trophy, but he kept it to himself. He had originally planned to have the thing stuffed. Now all that was left were some snapshots and an iron bracelet with mysterious markings on it. Oh well, another fish story, as they say: *the one that got away.*

Testament of the Scribe

I am passing through a land that is not my home, yet is hauntingly familiar to me, for surely I sojourned here in another incarnation, and I am eager to move on, so abhorrent is the thought of lingering. However, some few persons whom I recognize as allies among the teeming throngs of hostile strangers persuade me to tarry here a while longer, appealing to my most lamentable spiritual weakness, an inordinate artistic pride, placing in my hands thick sheaves of antique papers, illuminated codices that once I scrawled in my wasted youth—rare narratives of which I've forgotten the substance, although the penmanship is undeniably mine. Succumbing to vanity, I begin to sign these anonymous works, marveling at the ornate lurid decorations I had emblazoned on each sheet, and then I hesitate, wondering if I really ought to keep these lost relics of my past, if I dare claim them at last and add them to my store of accomplishments, but after scanning a particularly provocative passage, I recall why I had abandoned these pernicious leaves in that other life I now disavow—remember the reason I had left them scattered across a wasteland whose air boasts the fragrance of a cloying tropical sweetness and whose days are tempered by dissolute warmth: for these pages are songs of an irredeemable decadence, verses of a feverish degeneracy, and I shall not risk acknowledging them nor take pride in having fashioned what is undeniably an instrument of my own damnation.

139

And I become aware of shadowy figures now gathering on the periphery of the metropolis; the reckless arrogance of an impure heart always draws them forth.

The pages slip from my hands, they flutter and fall from the parapet on which I stand atop this rocky precipice, undulating like autumn leaves down the face of the walls and onto the waters below where their decaying husks will soon clot the drains.

"Will you not sign?" my companions plead. "Will you not affix your name to these documents and own the truths they embody?"

"No!" I proclaim as I pull away from their grasp. "I reject these abominable works! I denounce them as lies and vile seductions!"

Sensing I will not be further detained, my erstwhile companions allow me to depart and instead turn to gathering what few pages I have not already tossed to the winds, believing them worthy of their veneration. I leave them to their foolish task, noticing as I place distance between us that certain stern beings well known to me have emerged as they will in such circumstances and are moving in stealthily from the dusky fringes of the hilltop enclave, murder burning brightly in their eyes, while others of this hooded tribe break away to follow me as they always have, insuring thus my continued wandering, for it is only through a resolute dedication to ceaseless movement and the rejection of all worldly vanities that I have been able thus far to escape the inevitable terrible reckoning these sanctified ones seek to deliver.

And now, above and behind me, from the crimson-stained streets of the high city come echoing anguished cries of mortal agony—the ultimate gasps of those unfortunates whose favor I had foolishly curried before I regained my composure and resumed my solitary pilgrimage.

PART 4

WITCHES AT SUNSET

OBLIVION'S DAUGHTER

On these languid summer evenings, I press my face against the window screen, lean into the taunting wind and breathe deep of night's rich effluvia, an intoxicating blend of the vague scent of occulted animals that desperately elude you and the riotous exhalations of your pallid garden flowers. Those terrorized creatures, your inevitable prey, have fled to the hills, vainly hopeful of escaping your grasp, while the lurid flowers, with no history of catastrophe among their race, playfully call out to you in dulcet feminine strains of song, tempting you, begging you to inhale their strong aromas, to touch the honeyed stickiness of their bee-luring stigma. I greedily flood my nostrils with this sweet nocturnal fluid, and know that I have arrived in the eternal night, standing on the dizzy brink of infinite darkness, surveying the legion sinister joys that oblivion holds, and while the only lights I see are the pale pulsations of remote stars burning down through the eons in the borderless realms of Heaven, in my mind's eye I see you, radiant child, preparing your luxuriant chamber for my reception in the vaults subterrene, in your caverns draped with carmine silk, inviting me entry to the blood-drenched vacuity of your limitless want.

AGENTS OF DREAD

I have heard the ghost children
laughing down through night's depths,
long after midnight sighs,
when a mournful wind
carries their feral scent to me,
and in terror I have shuttered my windows
and marked the door posts and lintels
with ruddy sigils to bar their entrance,
and yet still they arrive, two
emaciated young girls with stringy hair
and pale, ashen skin,
garbed in decayed raiment,
begging admittance with
fey voices and dead obsidian eyes,
appealing to my sympathetic instincts,
singing "Oh sir, we hunger
and it is time to feed!" and
"Permit us entry, sir! We are cold and
your chamber exudes warmth!" But,
I do not give in to this demonic pair;
I remain vigilant, for
I have viewed the ghastly remains
of kindhearted innocents
who made the fatal error
of unbolting their doors and
admitting fiends who would

feast on bodies and souls
in the guise of benign children
with ebony eyes and
razor-sharp teeth.

THE WITCH POOL

Once a week Derrick Horus treated himself to a caffè mocha at the Hobo Bean Coffee Company. Sure, it was ridiculously overpriced at $3.50, consisting merely of a shot of espresso, a squirt of steamed milk, a dash of vanilla extract, a dollop of cocoa powder, and a swirl of whipped cream on top with a sprinkling of cinnamon, but it tasted so damned good that he couldn't resist indulging in one on a regular basis, regardless of the admittedly unhealthful nature of the drink with its high fat and sugar content. It wasn't like one of these now and then all by itself would be enough to clog his arteries, nor would he live forever anyway, even if his diet was perfect. *You have to live a little,* he told himself. *None of us will be here forever.* He took a cautious sip of the hot beverage and savored the richness of the creamy concoction in his mouth, narrowing his eyes against the bright rays of the afternoon sun as they streamed through the gaps in the shop's front window blinds. At sixty-eight, his auburn hair was thinning on top, and he walked with a slight limp, yet he was still a handsome man and in relatively decent shape. He had a few good years left—or at least he hoped as much.

Spread out before him on the table was a copy of *The Advertiser.* His cane was propped up against the edge of the table a few inches from his right hand, at the ready. An article on page six had his attention. It concerned an alleged coven of modern-day witches who supposedly performed "dark rites in isolated pastures" in the lonesome hills behind Arkham. A few hysterical citizens claimed these women were responsible for the recent disappearances of a large number of cats in the city, but that hardly seemed likely to Derrick. No doubt the alleged "witches" were simply so-called "pagans" who were more or less innocently cavorting about naked in nature, or whatever, secluded from the judgmental eyes of Arkham's more uptight denizens. And maybe they smoked a little weed while they danced around—who really cared? *Live and let live* was his motto. He was fairly familiar with that hilltop location, and it was indeed a peaceful, pleasant vantage spot from which to survey the city's many unique districts. He had gone up there a number of times when he was in his early twenties, in the company of a charming young lady who was quite free with her favors. The thought of her immediately brought to mind a series of pleasant romantic memories, but his dreamlike reverie was abruptly interrupted when he suddenly realized that an unusual-looking stranger was rapidly approaching his table.

The intruder was someone that he cursorily judged to be an uncommonly attractive older woman: tall, lithe, even willowy. But at second glance, her leanness was so extreme that it bordered on an unwholesome gauntness. A decidedly mature woman, she was still in command of a definite feminine allure, despite the fact that she was easily within a year or two of his own age. With long raven-black hair that was streaked with silver, and wearing a lengthy black dress and—despite the heat of the day—a red crocheted shawl and a floppy, wide-brimmed black hat, she had the air of a relic of the Sixties: a once-beautiful hippie girl who had sadly gone to seed. Derrick was used to seeing her kind in the Hobo Bean. The clientele had always been a mix of college kids from nearby Miskatonic University and older bohemian types—painters, poets, and other oddballs. She must be one of the latter. He didn't think he'd seen her before, however; she was eccentric enough—even intriguing in an unlikely way—that he would have remembered her. She was coming straight at him, there was no doubt about that. He prepared to be interrupted.

He laughed to himself when he realized that he had never looked at older women this way when he was younger; they were all categorically beneath consideration as potential partners. But once he hit sixty, he started looking at them differently—more carefully, more generously—and surprisingly began to find some of them more appealing than he once would have imagined. It was a matter of adjusting one's standards. Or, simply a case of being realistic. There was no way he could attract the type of women he once had, before the years had begun to wear on him. Now, he took what he could find in the way of love. Besides, their experience made many of these older women more pleasant to be around. They were less self-involved than younger women, and more accepting of minor flaws in the men with whom they associated. Yes, he could possibly be interested in this one, although she looked like she might be somewhat deranged.

"Madame," he nodded. "May I help you?"

"Yes, and yourself as well in the process, good sir. May I?" she gestured inquiringly to the empty wire frame chair across from him.

"Certainly. Be my guest." He nodded again and gestured with his right hand to indicate that she was welcome to join him.

"Thank you kindly," she said, her voice high and raspy. She had been carrying a hot drink in a take-out cup which she now placed on the table before her. *Decaf tea,* he guessed. She looked as if strong coffee might kill her. *Physically fragile but strong of spirit.* "I noticed you perusing that piece in the newspaper about goings-on in the pastures above Arkham," she continued, "and the alliance of exceptional ladies who gather there on occasion."

"Indeed, I was reading precisely that piece. It's quite engrossing, although I suspect the reporter was having his leg

149

pulled to some extent by the usual gang of troublemakers in our highly contentious community. I sincerely doubt that anything terribly wicked is going on up there beyond the routine sorts of high jinx engaged in by the more adventuresome members of the local New Age coterie."

"*Au contraire.* The actual situation up there is indeed as reported. I know that for a fact. Not the nonsense about missing cats—good grief! How silly!—but the haggish nature of the secret assemblies. That part is totally true. Witches gather there on nights when the moon is full—such as tonight. Under the sailing clouds they disrobe and form a circle of trust, the 'Ring of Sisterhood' they call it, and they dance freely to an enchanted tune that is piped by their clever familiars, those small, furry beings who hide from conventional men and women in the depths of the desolate woods. It is a wonder and a sight to behold! You would love it, I know. You really would!"

She seemed quite certain of this latter claim, as if she had known him for years. He wondered if she was dangerous. He had known a few mentally unbalanced ladies, and they were always more trouble than they were worth. Should he flee without delay, or was she merely a harmless lunatic, a garden-variety space case?

Derrick gazed more deeply into her skillfully mascaraed eyes. They were so utterly intense: dark, vibrant pools of mystery and passion. Some ancient sentiment stirred within him. She leaned a bit closer and smiled slyly. That's when he noticed her unexpectedly enticing cleavage: her body was far firmer than the average woman of her age.

"You don't recognize me, do you, Derrick?"

His brow furled quizzically as he studied her face more closely.

"Should I? Have we met?"

"Oh, we've met, and then some!" she said in a lilting voice that was almost girlish.

He stared harder, and still did not recognize her. And then, suddenly, *he did.* She was the very same woman with whom he had visited the high pastures above Arkham so many years ago. A half a century ago, in fact.

"Jesus Christ."

"Hardly. More like Mary Magdalene, at least according to the early church fathers who so groundlessly slandered her, calling her a prostitute and all that nonsense."

"Alanna Brellome. I can't believe it's you. How on earth did you find me? And how did you know it was me? I've changed since those days. It's a miracle you were able to identify me after all this time."

"No, not a miracle at all. I never really stopped watching you after we parted ways. Discreetly, of course. I kept my distance. But I always followed your movements, kept up with the developments in your life. Kind of like a stalker," she laughed.

"And now, after all this time, you've finally come forward, and reconnected with me. Stepped out of the shadows and revealed yourself. But why? Why now?"

"Because *it's time,* Derrick E. Horus! Time for us to return to the hills behind Arkham, to resume our former lovemaking. To shed our inhibitions once more. To slough off this weary flesh, cast aside these frail, exhausted bodies. To step out into the moonlight, naked and free. Time for our new lives to begin— together!"

*

That evening, against his better judgment, Derrick did as she had requested before leaving him at the café to resume reading his newspaper. That was to go to an address she had written on the back of a business card (not hers), where he found a derelict two-story Victorian house occupying the last lot on an abandoned street. Climbing the dilapidated wooden stairs, he found the front door wide open and entered with a degree of trepidation. Alanna was sitting at a small table, facing him, the tall candle before her causing her face to glow in the otherwise dark parlor. Cards were spread out before her—a Tarot deck, perhaps. Her hands were placed palms-down on the tabletop, fingers spread wide, arms with locked elbows positioned on either side of her. She seemed surprised that he had actually come, although he had promised he would. Without hesitation she rose from her chair, and he saw that she still wore the black dress, shawl, and hat from earlier in the day. Despite the gloominess of the scene, he detected a warm smile playing across her lips. As he approached her, his cane tapping rhythmically along the bare hardwood floor, she likewise walked toward him, and when they met, she kissed him seductively on the mouth. He had not been kissed like that in a very long time and was amazed at the tenderness of it. Tears filled his eyes.

"I'm … I'm sorry," he muttered in what he hoped was a manly tone. "It's just that … well, I'm afraid I will disappoint you. I'm not the man I was when we were last together."

"Impossible," she said with such conviction that he could not help but be reassured. "I shall not be disappointed; you have my word for it. Your presence is all that I desire, sir, and all that I had hoped for. That you are with me, again, is my wish fulfilled. Anything beyond the joy of this moment is unexpected, and for it I can only be grateful. Now come with me to the wonders on the hill." And with that, she led him by the hand, out the front door, and down the stairs. From there, they hurried along the crumbling sidewalk until it ended, then trudged up a footpath on the side of a hill as quickly as he could manage given his bad leg, eventually reaching the plateau. Soon they were roaming the pastures overlooking Arkham and came to the precise place that had been written about in *The Advertiser:* a broad, grassy meadow, over which a thin layer of mist drifted. High above, the luminous moon had turned the surrounding clouds a pearly white. He spotted a circle of stones in the midst of the pasture. At its heart stood a firepit, its heaps of ashes lifeless. *This must be where the enchantresses gather,* he mused to himself.

"Yes, I know what you must be thinking, and your hunch is correct. It is here we witches dance when we pay homage to Luna, our moon goddess, and I pray you will join us in the frolic soon to be performed. But first, you and I have something very important to do. For we are to be *transformed,* my good sir."

Out of the corner of his eye Derrick detected some movement off to his left. Deep within in a dense patch of trees lining the edge of the pasture a number of dark forms moved about in the shadows: women in long black dresses like the one being worn by Alanna. Some had tall conical hats. It seemed incredible to him that contemporary witches still dressed like that, in the archaic manner of their historic predecessors. It looked so old-fashioned, and yet, there they were, milling about ominously a short distance from him. He detected smaller forms accompanying some of them, a bizarre assortment of animals including cats, pigs, dogs, owls, rabbits, and others. Smaller creatures like birds, toads, snakes, and mice the witches cradled in their arms or carried perched on their shoulders and heads. *Those must be their familiar spirits,* thought Derrick. The crones were gathering for the coming ritual, the dark rite they would execute in homage to their lunar goddess. Fantastic, and yet he saw them with his own eyes.

Something about this situation disturbed Derrick. Were these women dangerous? Should he be frightened for his safety? He was alone there with them, greatly outnumbered. If the proceedings took an ugly turn, he would be entirely at their mercy.

And what about Alanna herself? Had she always practiced witchcraft? Thinking back, she had spoken vaguely to him about it a few times in the old days, never going into any detail, and he had assumed it was some frivolous game she played at, a passing

153

affectation. But apparently, it had been and continued to be a far more serious matter than that for her: a lifetime devotion. *What is she really up to? Should I be worried?* Maybe he should, but then, what did he have to lose at this point in his life?

"You can trust me, Derrick. Goodness alone will come of this dalliance." He looked into her radiant eyes and saw no evil there, only a remarkable joy, and it reminded him of the profound love and ecstatic pleasure they had shared when young.

He decided to give in to her, to submit, to allow her to work her magic. He would take his chances with the other witches.

By this time, the coven, still accompanied by their familiars, had emerged from their shadowy seclusion among the trees and were in the open pasture, chanting in unison as they walked toward the ring of stones at a slow, measured pace. The witch in front, an elderly crone with long, straggly gray hair, a bony pointed chin, and a narrow, hooked nose, seemed to be in charge. She began to chant in a low, guttural voice, and soon the others joined in. Derrick didn't recognize any of the words of their chant, whether they were some foreign tongue or an archaic form of English. As the assembly passed through the pasture, members bent over now and then to pick up twigs and branches and a few larger chunks of decaying wood from fallen trees: fuel for the fire they would build in the center of the stone ring. The lead hag carried a bag of dried mugwort herb, from which she pulled a tied bundle that she lit fire to and carried before her, waving it from side to side ceremoniously to ward off malevolent spirits and cleanse the air. Reaching the ring, she walked around it, the others following her until the entire coven was circled there. The lead crone made a sign with her hand, and all the witches threw the twigs and branches they had collected into a pile at the heart of the ring. Then she tossed several handfuls of loose dried herbs from her bag on top of the wood pile and ignited it with the tip of her burning smudge stick. At first, the pile only smoldered, but soon the kindling burst into yellow and red flames that licked up into the night air of the pasture toward the radiant moon above.

In the bright glow of the bonfire, the witches all began to strip themselves bare, unabashedly shedding their gowns, some letting them slip demurely to the ground in the manner of chaste maidens while others, more bold, flung them off lustily, and Derrick was startled to see the nude forms of the women as they cavorted about in the flickering firelight.

"The ritual has begun," declared Alanna. "My sisters are skyclad and turning with the rhythms of the night, ready to receive the blessings that flow down from the loving moon."

She chose that moment to take his hand and lead him into a copse set at the back of the high pasture, off to the right of the stone circle. Within this small stand of trees, hidden among the oaks, they came to a pool of silvery water enclosed by a ring of granite boulders. From there, they could still see the flickering bonfire through the trees behind them and passing before it, the silhouettes of cavorting witches as they danced in worship of their lunar mistress. The mist floating low above the ground within the copse was thicker than that in the rest of the meadow, and as Alanna and Derrick moved through it, clouds of vapor swirled about them in an enchanted manner. He inhaled, filling his lungs, and his nostrils tingled with the unusual aroma of some exotic incense that he was at a loss to identify: a pungent smell that was pleasurable, luxuriant, and highly seductive.

Derrick looked back again toward the bonfire and for the first time noticed there were many pairs of small, glowing eyes, all staring at him and Alanna. The eyes were all quite close to the ground, and soon he detected the ebon forms of their little bodies. The familiars had left the ritual being performed in the pasture and come over to watch them.

Did these strange creatures, who appeared to have some kind of supernatural symbiotic relationship with the women

155

of the coven, pose a threat to him, at least, if not to the both of them? Was their presence in the copse the witches' way of keeping a watchful eye on the errant couple while the women performed their magical ceremonies? He didn't know but found their unblinking stares unsettling.

One of the familiars—a mangy-looking weasel—stepped nearer to Derrick and bared its sharp teeth while hissing at him. The malignant creature's eyes burned with pure hatred. Did this portend hostility on its part? His grip tightened on the handle of his cane, thinking he could use it as a weapon if any of the animals attacked him. Let them try; he would bash in their brains.

Alanna saw this mounting tension but seemed to pay it no mind. Drawing close to him, she grasped both of Derrick's hands in hers and peered deeply into his eyes, uttering fervently, "All during the many years that have passed since we ceased being lovers, I always planned to bring you to this spot someday, knowing that ultimately a singular night would come when we were both old and death was not far away, and on that night we would be reunited, and I would show you how we could slough off our old bodies and take up new ones. Young and fresh bodies—fully alive—essentially the same material forms we had occupied back then, when we were first together. You remember how wonderful it was when we made love in these hills under the moonlight? Now is that special night, Derrick! A second life awaits us. All we need do is to walk into the pool, and it will refresh us and renew our forms. Follow me!"

"Yes," he said, entranced by her ageless eyes and doing his best to ignore his nagging fears about the reveling witches and their aggressive familiars. "I will follow you."

Those fears included legends he had heard about terrible deeds done by outlaw covens, including acts of blood sacrifice involving animals and even, on rare occasions, human victims. He put these doubts out of his mind and thought only of Alanna and her charms—both now and when she was young.

She smiled regally then took several steps toward the pool, shedding her hat, shawl, and gown until she was completely nude, her slender figure pale in the moonlight. The sparkling mist clung to her lovely yet timeworn being. A few feet farther, and she entered the pool, walking forward until the water was up to her knees, then her slender waist, then her neck. She turned again toward Derrick and nodded, as if to say, *Come join me*. And he did. As he neared the pool's edge, she took a few more steps toward its center, sinking deeper into the water until her head disappeared. Then, as he continued walking into the pool, she began to emerge from it, and as the rivulets of liquid silver streamed down her wet physique, Derrick saw that she had spoken the truth, for she was the *other* Alanna he had known and loved in the distant past—a twenty-year-old woman in the prime of her life. Eager to join her in this new incarnation, Derrick waded farther into the opalescent waters and began to feel all the weariness and pain and sorrow of a lifetime falling away from his inner core. One additional step, and his head was below the surface. The last thing he heard before going under was Alanna's jubilant laughter—the clear, lush tones of her girlish voice.

Fully submerged in the pool, Derrick was plunged into a liquid realm of near silence, no longer hearing the chanting of the witches, the crackling of the bonfire, nor the hissing of the vicious weasel. The only sound remaining was the soft burbling of air bubbles as his limbs treaded the water to keep him from sinking to the bottom. In a matter of seconds, the pool bestowed its promised magic upon his body. A new vigor coursed through his entire being, making his muscles feel incredibly stronger, his flesh amazingly leaner, his posture as erect as a lad's. All weakness and soreness was gone from his frame, and he literally felt like a new man—a youthful one.

157

His head broke the pool's surface, and he walked out of it and onto the solid earth of the shore. A few feet away lay his cast-aside cane; he didn't need it anymore. Beautiful Alanna stood before him, her alluring smile welcoming him to what he prayed would be a new life for them. And in the dark copse behind her, he saw the many glowing eyes of the still-menacing familiars staring ravenously at him, beyond which he glimpsed between the oaks the silhouettes of the now ecstatic witches, chanting and cavorting wildly before the high-rising flames of their ritualistic bonfire.

But in the foreground Derrick saw with unexplainable horror the fiercely glaring weasel—which he somehow intuited was Alanna's personal familiar—as it raised a set of reed pipes to its nasty mouth and began to play a haunting tune in accompaniment to the witches' frenzied dancing.

Three weeks later

The dining area at the front of the Hobo Bean was unusually crowded that afternoon, so rather than wait ten or fifteen minutes for a vacant table there, Alanna Brellome scanned the far wall of the coffee shop for an open place to sit at one of the smaller tables. There was but one: an empty chair at a table positioned under a rather grotesque vintage poster advertising a Mexican horror film. She would have to share the table with a solitary older gentleman, but that was okay. She had actually known him many years ago, when for the better part of a summer they had conducted a torrid love affair that at its heights featured remarkable nights of passion in the isolated hills behind Arkham. Carrying her cup of hot tea carefully so as not to spill any, she made her way toward him, a seductive smile playing upon her lips. The man had been engrossed in the morning edition of the *Arkham Advertiser,* and as he looked up to meet her gaze with a puzzled look on his face, he lowered the newspaper and she saw that he had been reading the lead story with its regrettably sensationalistic headline: *Local Man's Remains Found at Alleged Hilltop Cult Site.*

His befuddled expression told her that he found her fairly attractive and perhaps even vaguely familiar but did not yet consciously recognize her. Alanna knew that he would remember her, fondly, once they began talking.

"Is this seat taken, sir?" she inquired in a convincingly innocent tone.

"Not at all," he said, his face suddenly flushed. "By all means, madam, please join me."

Song for Naughty Children

The king was in the charnel house,
Stacking up his mummies;
The queen was in the abattoir,
Smashing straw-head dummies.

The maid was in the sepulchre,
Pulling off her dress,
When wandered in a dog-faced ghoul;
He made an awful mess.

Sing a song of cosmic dread.
The Queen called forth her slaves
And singing as she slit their throats,
She laid them in their graves.

When the tombs were opened,
The dead began to moan.
Then four-and-twenty skeletons
Restored him to the throne.

Upon the Night Ether

We dead listen in during the long, post-midnight hours, monitoring your radio broadcasts, gleaning snatches of life, glimmerings of color enhanced by emotion, vicarious romance and the semblance of a long-dead vitality. We drain the feeble life juices from the radio waves wafting in upon the night ether, milk the life forces from the oscillating voice vibrations. Little do you know what we work at, toil at in the lost hours of your heavy dreaming. Little suspect you the myriad ways in which we dead rob you of your life force, suck it from the very marrow of your earthly flesh. Soon enough you will join us here in the bleak netherworld of the dead. Soon enough will you join us in our nefarious endeavors. Have you speculated upon the possibility of raising the spectre of our shadow forms from the dust of the ages? It may be done. But be wary; we rise with borrowed life energies, taken from the sleeping forms of your most beloved ones. Better for you to break this contact between the dual regions, sever the channels between the dimensions. Not enough to close the cursed tome and utter no more the spells of the necromancers; you must cease as well the radiations you emit; we listen in during the gloomy early morning hours, when all is still and communication between the spheres is most possible. We reach out—extending tendrils of negative energy across the incalculable chasms of space and time—and touch, and drain that which you thought sacred, inviolable.

We feed upon the harmonies we find in blood and tissue and bone. We rise up from our charnel beds and breathe new atmosphere into aeon-dried lungs. Strange fire illuminates our rotted eyes; weird ululations issue forth from our parched, papery black lips. We move again with the semblance of life—a false, whorish mockery of life—and we prepare a place for you beside us in our eternal charnel homes. And some night soon, you too shall listen in to the sounds of life that waft in upon the night ether, the sounds of life that shall confuse you with their raw vitality, that shall awaken long dead memories, that shall make you rise from troubled sleep of ages and extend long tendrils through the vaults of cosmic waste to touch—so gently, so unlovingly—that which sleeps, which breathes, in the heavy dreams of life.

THE MILK HARE

A dancing witch I spy beneath the moon,
In gauzy gown that slips from shoulders bare.
While singing verses unadorned by tune,
Her shrill voice resonates the silvered air.
Entranced, I follow her into the weald
And thicket deep where she prepares the hare
Who does her bidding when the pact is sealed,
So that the dame may take of milk her share.

A rabbit formed of sticks and drops of blood,
The beldame's kiss arouses it to life.
She gives her oath that it will suck the cow,
Yet morning finds me lying in the mud,
A fool for having followed this false wife;
Bereft of milk, the witch I disavow.

Lines Written in the Night Wind

Night is forgiving; I welcome it, and wish the day would never return, for with the darkness comes forgetfulness, tender as a mother's love, all-merciful, the lurid yellow poppies oozing a sleep-inducing narcotic, their moist petals pressed like pulpy lips against the ancient hand-blown panes. It seems the past is sloughed off, shed like an old skin, carried away on silent, undulant waves over shadowed rolling hills. It is only now, after the falling away of cruel iron restraints, that secrets become apparitions, eagerly phosphorescent. The startled eye beholds their unlikely image a moment too long, then loses it in the murky haze. It is the hour when all the world's artifice becomes unhinged ... the day-lit verities a pale memory. Would this darkness but stay, I might thrive like these flowers, and dream forever without words, by the dark flowing waters of oblivion.

A FRENZY OF WITCHES

When the witches had enough
Of eating children on the bluff,
They descended to the village,
There to further kill and pillage—
Slashing throats and bashing heads,
Torching clergy in their beds,
Casting spells on all they hated,
Till their violent lusts were sated.

Done, they fell upon their knees,
Each as pious as you please.
Begged absolution from the Goat,
Who cloaked each crone in his black coat.
All returned then to the hills,
Boasting of their arcane thrills.

ALONG THAT PALLID PATH

Oddly, thought Frank in retrospect long after the vacation had ended, although thousands of devoted acolytes toured the historic Cindy Silk homestead each year, very few of them made the side trip to the nearby city cemetery where Ms. Silk's mortal remains were buried. This may have been due to the utter lack of publicity afforded to the gravesite, whereas the home of the celebrated nineteenth-century author had become a major tourist destination in the region. The fact that the graveyard was rather difficult to locate surely played a role in further limiting the number of people who ultimately succeeded in paying their respects at the Silk family plot. Given the scant number of visitors, the graveyard was inconsistently maintained, with outlying areas containing the more obscure plots having been abandoned to high grass and weeds, and its poor condition didn't exactly make the cemetery an appealing place to visit. Or, maybe there was a more sinister reason why almost nobody visited the grave site.

Guided tours of the Cindy Noemi Silk residence were offered daily from April through September, with summer being the busiest season. Frank Wynn and his wife, Mercy, chose the early fall for their first trip there. This was their fourth vacation in New England but the first one in which the itinerary included time in Amherst. The weather was fine during their week-long trip—warm and sunny every day—but thankfully the crowds of

July and August had thinned to a mere trickle. They found the Silk home easily, it being only a half-mile drive from their hotel. Frank parked the rental car on the street in front of the property, and they were the first members of the public admitted when the gates opened at 10 a.m. Frank was immediately glad they had come early, as there was only one other couple in line for the first tour, and their guide—a gentleman who was an expert on the poetry of Cindy Silk and had written a book about her—told them they could ignore the "no photography" signs posted behind the front desk and take a few pictures, as long as they did so while his back was turned and he was "looking the other way."

Frank's emotional response to finally being in Cindy's house after a lifetime of studying her work was strong and immediate. The moment he passed through the back porch area which served as the public entrance and into the home proper, a wave of joy spread throughout his entire body, and he swore to himself that he could almost sense her presence there beside him; tears flooded his eyes. Being reserved and easily embarrassed, he was relieved that the rest of their group was in front of him and couldn't see his flushed face.

The tour lasted an hour and a half, during which they spent time in nearly all the rooms of the two houses which formed the homestead. The main house was Cindy's father's home, called "The Estate." Her older brother Philbrick's house was next door and was known as "Perennial Firs." A footpath had been worn into the grassy meadow separating the two houses, the result of original members of the household and then later tourists walking between the homes countless times every day for the past century and a half. Mercy, who, like her husband, had a lifelong fascination with the famous poet and read everything she could lay her hands on about Silk, told Frank that Cindy loved this serene path and would mentally compose her rhymes while strolling along its course. Mercy was thrilled just to be walking the same path as Silk had.

After the tour had officially concluded, Frank and Mercy parted with the guide at The Estate and walked by themselves back and forth between the two houses several times, trying to imagine what it must have been like for Silk to spend most of her life at the homestead, seldom leaving the small town. Frank stared down at his shoes as he walked along, picturing in his mind Cindy Silk's delicate feet, clad in the slippers they had seen in her upstairs bedroom, taking one step and then another and another upon the carpeting of leaves and twigs that littered the path.

Before they left the property, they re-entered the back porch and bought a few items in the gift shop, including a copy of the tour guide's book. The guide was standing nearby, and Mercy asked if he would mind inscribing and signing it to her, which he graciously did, although Frank was mildly annoyed by the fact that the man—who was obviously not a bibliophile—badly mangled the cover of the paperbound volume when he forced it to open wider than the tight binding was designed to go and then pressed the open book flat against the surface of the sales counter before taking out his pen and writing on the title page in a shaky, barely legible hand.

From the homestead they drove into historic downtown Amherst and found a popular restaurant they had read about in one of the tour guides. In Silk's day the building had been a mercantile store but now served as a stylish eatery catering to the tourist trade. They took a table by the windows and ordered from the waitress: a Caesar salad with chicken and a soda for Mercy, and a bowl of mac and cheese and coffee for Frank. The food arrived faster than Frank expected.

"This is the best mac and cheese I've ever tasted," announced Frank.

"Really?"

"Absolutely."

"So what did you think of the houses? Did they meet your expectations?" asked Mercy.

"Wonderful, both of them. They're quite different from one another, of course."

"They are." Mercy always ate much faster than Frank did and was already half done with her salad, whereas he had only taken two bites of his meal.

"I really felt a sense of Silk's presence in The Estate," continued Frank. "It's a more modest home than her brother's, reflecting her father's strict and somber traditional Calvinist values. But in her bedroom—which served as her private sanctuary from all that churchy fire and brimstone gloominess around her—you can better feel the innate joyfulness with which she met life. You probably noticed that The Estate, being the more important of the two homes, has been extensively restored, parts of it updated to meet modern building codes, and while that's all well and good, it creates a certain disconnect between what the place had been when she lived there and what we now experience in touring it. I kind of wish they had just left it alone aside from maintaining it. Preserve it, sure, but don't refurbish everything."

"Yeah, I agree," nodded Mercy between bites. "The Perennial Firs is much more original and untouched. It's like the last living Silk family member moved out sometime in the early twentieth century, and nothing has really changed since then. It has the original wallpaper—peeling in places—and original paint on the walls, with soot stains and cracks in the plaster and some lighter-colored areas where paintings have been temporarily removed for cleaning, and even the fancy old furniture and art is completely original. It's eerie how little in there has changed. Kind of like an abandoned museum."

"Or a mausoleum."

"All the time we were there I felt like Cindy and Philbrick and a bunch of their friends would walk into the room at any moment."

"Me too."

Mercy was already finished with her lunch. She pulled a guidebook out of her purse and began rereading the part about how to find the Silk family plot at the cemetery.

"Give me a minute or two, I'm almost done," he said, sipping his coffee, although in reality half of his meal remained to be eaten.

*

The cemetery was not as easy to locate as the guidebook had said it would be. Following one of the recommended routes, they turned down an alley that was supposed to lead to a cemetery rear gate but instead dead-ended behind a run-down gas station. The graveyard was nowhere in sight from there. Another route—to an alleged side gate—instead brought them to a row of small shops, again with no cemetery in view. Approaching from yet another angle, they drove to the area where the main entrance to the cemetery was supposed to be located but saw only block after block of stately old homes, with no gate to be found. They were about to give up when—in a random act of desperation—Frank pulled into a parking lot on the side of an apartment building, and behind the last row of cars found a chain-link fence with an unmarked gate giving access into what he first thought was a vacant lot overgrown with weeds.

"This is it!" said Mercy, opening her car door.

"You really think so?"

"Yes. Look back there, among the trees. Those are tombstones!"

"Damn, you're right. Let's go!"

They tried the gate and found it unlocked. The remnants of a dirt path led away into the weeds. Feeling adventuresome, they followed it, hoping it would lead to Cindy Silk's grave. Once

171

they had passed through the stand of trees, the graveyard began to look less abandoned and wild, although it was still far from presentable. Some semblance of order began to be apparent, with fewer of the headstones being knocked over, flat on the ground, or perilously tilted to one side. Farther on, they entered an area that actually seemed well-groomed, as if someone still cared about honoring the memory of the departed souls buried there. Oddly, thought Frank, the two of them seemed to be entirely alone there. Or so he thought at the time.

"Where is everyone?" asked Mercy, looking around.

"My exact thought," replied Frank. "Although, considering how hard this place is to find, I'm really not surprised that no one is here but us."

They realized they had reached the main part of the burial ground. A narrow service road wound through the center of it. The small, ancient, crumbling tombstones that had been so prevalent in the overgrown periphery they had just passed through gave way to taller monuments in decent condition, some of them in the form of impressive obelisks. At the end of the road Frank spotted a stately home marking the cemetery's edge, but there was still no sign of an entrance. Mercy was fifty feet ahead of him. She had come upon a family plot with four large headstones enclosed within a black wrought-iron fence.

"This is it, Cindy Silk's grave," she called back to him. He walked faster than normal to catch up with her. She was standing by an ornate chest-high gate on the side of the enclosure closest to the road. It was locked and bore a brass plaque inscribed with the words "In Memory of Poetess Cindy Silk" and "Erected by the Silk Kinsfolk on August 28, 1955." Although Mercy had already tried it, Frank shook the gate again to make sure that it was really locked. They walked around to the side where the Silk headstones were lined up. One was Cindy's, another was her sister Hope's. The third stone bore the names of her father and mother, and the fourth was that of her grandparents. A number of mementos had been left atop Cindy's headstone by visitors paying tribute to her. These included stones, seashells, and in one case, a vial of French perfume. Frank found these humble gestures by her fans quite touching. It was as if they were attempting to make personal contact with her, believing that some remnant of her mind or spirit lingered at the grave. He wondered if it were even possible that she could have some enduring presence in the place where her remains had been laid to rest, and at the same time haunt—so to speak—the homestead where she passed so many of her days and nights while alive.

Simultaneously, Mercy and Frank reached through the gap between the iron bars and touched Cindy's headstone. "Rest in peace, sweet Cindy," whispered Mercy.

"Amen to that," uttered Frank.

At that exact moment Frank noticed a strange, filthy, long-haired, wild-eyed man in ragged clothes a few rows away, dancing eerily among the graves. He didn't know why, but Frank's immediate impression was that the guy was some whacked-out male witch, obviously a vagrant, and possibly a physical threat to them. The man didn't seem to notice them watching him.

"Check him out," whispered Frank.

"Creepy," Mercy whispered back.

Frank tugged at Mercy's arm and led her back to a spot near the gate to the Silk family plot where they would be out of the man's direct line of vision, hidden behind a tall obelisk that rose halfway between him and them.

"What the hell is he doing?" she asked.

"Tripping out on drugs, or dancing? Maybe he's mentally ill," replied Frank. "Why is he flapping his arms like that? It's so weird!"

The man was lifting his outspread arms and then letting them fall in a gesture that resembled the mating ritual of a gigantic bird. His arm motions were quite slow—not as if he were actually

173

trying to fly, but more like he wanted to create air turbulence around the grave—and he stomped around in tight circles while flapping his arms.

"This is scaring me," said Mercy, a note of panic in her voice.

"Maybe he's performing some occult rite, trying to raise the dead."

"Whatever. Jesus Christ! Let's leave," she urged—a bit too loudly, thought Frank.

Suddenly the man turned to them as if he had heard her, but Frank pulled Mercy back and they were hidden behind the intervening obelisk before the guy spotted her.

"Not so loud!" he faintly hissed.

Her eyes were wide with fear as she silently mouthed the words *Let's go ... now!*

Wait until it's safe, he mouthed back, physically restraining her from bolting away and attracting the guy's attention.

Not seeing anyone around him, the man resumed his shamanic dance. For a while he was still turned in their general direction, flapping his arms, the ragged streamers of his torn shirt almost resembling feathers. Then, as he transitioned to a more trance-like state, the man began to stamp his bare feet in a tighter circle, turning away from them.

At that moment, Frank grabbed Mercy's hand and urgently led her back down the service road and into the stand of trees. Half running, half walking as fast as he could while still maintaining silence, Frank looked over his shoulder and was reassured to see that the crazy vagrant was still swooping around the same cluster of graves where they had first noticed him, not far from Cindy Silk's burial site. As soon as they were deep in the overgrown portion of the cemetery and completely out of the man's sight, they ran full-speed down the dirt path toward the gate where they had first entered the cemetery. Soon they reached the relative safety of the gate, and beyond it, their parked car.

"Hurry up!" pleaded Mercy as Frank fumbled in his pocket for his keys.

"Don't worry. I don't think he followed us. He's probably still back there doing his crazy witch-doctor thing."

But he wasn't.

They jumped in the car, Frank fired up the engine and backed out of the parking spot. As he shifted into drive, Frank glanced in the rear view mirror to see the wild man standing at the gate they had just scrambled through, staring at them with insane eyes.

The Warlock didn't need to physically follow Frank and Mercy to know where they went next. He watched them in his mind's eye as he returned to his rituals in the cemetery.

First, they went to a trendy café for the kind of rich, highly flavored coffee drinks he could never afford. When he did buy coffee, it was for a dollar at the convenience store, purchased with a handful of coins taken from among the mementos left behind by tourists on Cindy Silk's gravestone. He knew they were talking about him as they sipped their posh drinks, saying insulting things about his unkempt appearance and—to them—strange behavior. Little did they suspect the powers he held over the many souls that had been laid to rest in the historic cemetery. Power over even the wraith of the world-famous poet, Cindy Silk. They did not discern, nor could they suspect, that she again walked the footpath between the two Silk family homes, thanks to his having lifted her up from the cold oblivion of the Dead and breathed new animation into her withered form. Nor did they appreciate that she strolled the cemetery grounds, lost in melancholia, only because he had returned her to a somber semblance of life.

175

After the couple wearied of verbally abusing him, their inane chatter turned to other banal topics, such as how they would spend their afternoon—the last one in this town before they returned home the next day. Do what they might during those few remaining hours in her domain, the oppressive influence of the resurrected Cindy and her malignant second life among the crumbling tombs would not fully leave them. Rather, it would haunt them for the rest of their stay.

Earlier that day the Warlock had immediately sensed it the moment Frank and Mercy had entered the cemetery, psychically watching as they walked through the untended parts, and then, as they had approached Cindy Silk's grave, he had observed the ghost of Cindy following along a short distance behind them. The Warlock had cast an obscuring veil over Frank and Mercy's perceptions, and they had been unable to detect Cindy's presence. Although they could not have suspected as much, the Warlock had been aware of the couple even before they had found the cemetery. He knew that Cindy's spirit first manifested itself in their presence when they entered her bedroom with the tour guide. They did not see her vaporous likeness then; he had blocked their perception of her. That was one of the Warlock's powers: to control who could or could not see Cindy's specter. He had elevated her from extinction, along with the souls of many others buried in that cemetery, and he decided who might witness her apparition and who would be oblivious to it. He did not allow the herd of tourists—fools, the lot of them—to see her, because he did not want the common masses to know that she haunted the homestead and town cemetery. If this couple detected her phantom, they would tell others of their ilk, and word of her haunting would spread like wildfire. The town would become overrun with thrill-seekers, amateur ghost-hunters, and a virtual army of idiots, all of them interfering with his vital work as necromancer. So the couple were not granted the gift of seeing Cindy's shade. However, he would leave them with a single phantasmal scare to ensure they would never return to the cemetery again.

Their afternoon outing completed, the Warlock psychically watched as Frank and Mercy drove to their hotel, where they would rest for an hour before going out again for dinner. He knew the place well; its dumpster often contained discarded food from the hotel restaurant. It was only a few blocks from the cemetery, a five-minute walk. He went there, his daily rituals having come to a satisfactory conclusion, and walked around the building until he sensed the location of their room on the second floor at the back of the building. He didn't need to enter the building and go upstairs to accomplish his goal. Merely being in sight of the room's window was enough.

Frank wasn't really sleeping. He was stretched out on his back, on top of the bed, with his shoes off and his eyes closed, but remained conscious. "Catching my second wind," is how he described it to Mercy.

"Mind if I turn on the TV?" she asked.

"Not at all. I'm just resting. Give me another half hour and I'll be ready to go again."

His mind was peaceful at first. He ignored the babble of the program and instead thought of all they had seen and done that day. It had all lived up to his expectations. Maybe even exceeded them.

But then, something appeared in his field of vision: a roiling circle of bright colors and angular shapes where there should have been only the dull, ruddy murkiness of subdued daylight penetrating the blood vessel-laced flesh of his eyelids.

The seething mass of forms bound within the glowing sphere began to resolve itself into a cluster of distinct, identifiable shapes,

177

and what Frank saw there deeply disturbed him. They looked like living snakes—writhing, squirming, constantly moving—and then they morphed into countless grotesque heads at the end of long, snake-like necks that constantly rose and sank out of the mass, popping up and then darting back down, each face more obscenely demonic-looking than the last one.

What the hell? thought Frank. Was this some subconscious replay of the disturbing emotions he had felt while watching the hippie witch doctor dancing in the cemetery? Or was it more serious than that? Had Frank somehow carried away an occult hex from that insane guy? Had the creep cast a spell on him?

Determined to shake it off, whatever it was, Frank opened his eyes and instead of the unsettling hallucination saw only the shadowed stucco of the ceiling. He wanted nothing whatsoever to do with whatever malevolent force was assaulting his consciousness. He would not give in to its power but would resolutely ignore it. As he rose from the bed, he decided he would never bring up the subject of the male witch again. If Mercy brought it up, he would politely answer her and then change the subject as quickly as possible without alerting her suspicions that something about the guy bothered Frank. Nor would he ever speak about their having visited the cemetery, how difficult it was to find, all of that. No, he would keep his thoughts and comments about the trip centered around the Silk homestead, how much they had enjoyed seeing the places where Cindy had lived and written her magnificent poems. After all, that was the only part really worth remembering, wasn't it? The rest he would forget as quickly as possible. If he and Mercy ever came here again, he would persuade her to skip the cemetery. *Seen it once, seen it a thousand times,* he would tell her. By the time they sat down to dinner at the Rebel Inn, the cemetery couldn't have been further from Frank's mind.

*

On their way out of town, Mercy asked if they could please stop by The Estate for a few minutes so she could walk the path between the houses one last time.

"Sure," said Frank, "We have plenty of time."

He waited in the car while Mercy walked up the lawn to the start of the path and began following it toward the Perennial Firs. The sun was setting behind The Estate, and the path was dappled with a golden haze of fading daylight. *Truly beautiful,* he reflected. He enjoyed watching Mercy leisurely stroll down the path, knowing how much she savored every moment she spent in Cindy Silk's world. Then something unusual caught Frank's attention. A slight breeze came up and stirred some of the fallen leaves behind Mercy, lifting them from the path into a spinning swirl of dancing leaves that followed behind Mercy as she walked along. It would approach her from behind and then fall away, approach again, fall away again, as if it were teasing her to turn around and discover its presence. This happened all the way down the path, and then, after she had turned around at the Firs, all the way back to The Estate, and Mercy never once noticed it. Frank wondered if this gentle display were the true spirit of Cindy as she had been in life, unencumbered by the evil sway of the Warlock— her free, unfettered, playful heart making its presence known to him, if not to Mercy herself? He realized he would never really know the answer to that question, but the thought alone brought him great pleasure.

THREE WITCHES

Three witches in a pasture stood—
one in a cape, one in a hood,
and one clad only
in the skin of a lonely
wolf who was slain
where the deacon's wife had lain
with the son of a farmer
who didn't mean to harm her.
Her sin declaimed aloud,
she was roundly disavowed.

The witch in a cape
grabbed a cat by the nape
deep in a wood
where the three witches stood,
and gave it to the witch
who was thought to be good.
That witch thrashed the cat
with a wooden baseball bat
then wandered wide in search
of a place to discard
puss's body bruised and scarred—
she chose a shuttered church.

In a glade three witches stood—
one was bad, one was good,

and one was either,
or perhaps she was neither.
They danced in a pasture
underneath the harvest moon,
singing praises to Hastur,
echoed by a distant loon.

There the witch in wolf's skin
pledged to revel and to sin,
embraced her deep affinity
for voluptuous iniquity,
swore to practice excess,
although it always left a mess.

This youngest of the crones
to be born of the goat,
with her silver-bladed knife
cut the farm boy's throat
and dumped his flesh and bones
in the town's deep murky moat
to avenge the deacon's wife
at the cost of his life.

Then traipsing across the hills,
all three sisters had their thrills

by cavorting with Pan's Son,
ties and buttons all undone,
and they sang a song to Hastur
as they twirled in the pasture.

Part 5

Victorian Tales

PAINTED LADIES

The old man lives alone
in the derelict Victorian mansion,
his wife having left him
so many years ago it's like
she never was there. He misses
his daughter more, and
although she's a grown woman now
with a life of her own, he keeps
her dolls on display,
lined up on a high shelf
in her former bedroom.

Loneliness marks his days and
casts long shadows over his evenings.
His only solace comes
when, in the wee hours,
gramophone music once more
echoes though the upstairs chambers
and the decorous shades
of girls who worked and died there
when it was the town whorehouse
a century ago or more
traipse merrily down the halls,
flickering candles in their hands,
on errands of pleasure and comfort
to gentlemen callers.

185

And, on those precious nights when
one ghostly tart or another
shambles into his room to
share his wintry bed.

RED WINE

The Italian restaurant had been at its present location for six months. Before that, it had occupied a nondescript storefront beside an abandoned bus terminal. The meal I enjoyed on that sultry summer evening was the occasion of my first visit to the establishment in its new premises, and while I was favorably impressed by the agreeableness of the décor, some of the appeal the place held for me must be attributed to the rich memories I have of the building back in the days when it functioned first as a laundry and then a country store. Most of the other diners were probably not aware that the modest-sized rectangular wooden structure was built in 1895, the laundry having been one of the town's first businesses. The latest occupant's quirky yet tasteful sense of design, with charming Victorian prints covering practically every inch of the crudely plastered and brightly painted walls, and casual, almost haphazard arrangements of unmatched pieces of antique furniture in every room, all contributed to the creation of a distinctive European ambiance such as you might encounter in a modest but reputable family restaurant in Florence or Verona. I felt instantly at ease sitting at a solitary table with my back to the window blinds, waiting for my dinner, alternately sipping ice water and red wine. The cold blast from the air conditioning, further circulated by the slow-turning ceiling fans, helped cool me off some, for it had been a scorcher—another day in an endless series of such days with temperatures reaching above a hundred degrees Fahrenheit. The peaceful atmosphere and the subtle pleasure of a glass of wine at day's end acted as a simple but effective antidote to the unpleasantness of modern life.

After several sips of wine that left my glass a little more than half full, and while waiting for the plate of spaghetti to be delivered to my table, I decided to look around. To my left was an arched doorway leading into a darkened room. This room, and fanciful thoughts of what it might contain, aroused a sense of expectant curiosity in me, so I walked over to the arch and peered inside, but did not enter. I was not disappointed. The chamber was richly furnished, with baroque flourishes on the crimson flocked wallpaper, a carved mahogany bar running along the right side, and plush, overstuffed chairs situated around low mahogany tables; it had the look of a secluded chamber in a private men's club. A morose-looking gentleman sat hunched over in one of the chairs. He glanced up at me sullenly and then returned to staring at the drink in his hand. No one else was in there. I liked this dark, lush room with its air of privacy and exclusivity. It reminded me of a similar one in which I had attended a secret meeting that took place over a century ago, a meeting at which the fate of hundreds of souls was decided. A room in which actions were taken which resulted in the flowing of veritable rivers of human blood. A room that was in this very same town, in a building that was razed decades ago.

After finishing my meal, I arose with my refilled wine glass, strolled in a leisurely manner past the arched doorway, and passed through the noisy bar and out into the back courtyard, where smoking was permitted. When you have the option of immortality, you don't worry about lung cancer. I lit a cigar and inhaled, narrowing my eyes to a slit as I glanced behind me toward the setting sun. No one had followed me out, and I was alone in the fenced courtyard.

On my left, the kitchen extended out behind the main part of the building. I could see a blur of activity inside through the steamy windows, with waiters carrying trays back and forth while behind them white-aproned dishwashers labored at towering piles of dishes. A young woman—whom I knew to be a cook—appeared briefly in view. She was only there for a second, then darted toward a door to the right of the windows and stepped out into the courtyard.

She turned in my direction, smiled in a friendly but not too forward way, as if to acknowledge my presence but not invite familiarity, then looked away. I nodded cordially in return.

Her name was Marie, and she took her break every evening at this time. I knew that and everything else about her: home address, names of friends and family, where she had gone to school, medical condition, romantic history—all that. Not to suggest that I had some unsavory interest in her; I didn't. It was just part of the record. She was next in line. When she reached a certain age, and I reached a certain point in my biological cycle, a transfer of vital life force would be made. I would be renewed, and she would expire. It had been arranged long ago. There was nothing personal about it. It was the system my kind had set up many years ago, in that building that was long since demolished.

I had known this from the beginning, from her birth. She was not aware of it.

This was the night on which it was fated she would be sacrificed so that I might live. It would not take very long; her break period was sufficient. It was to have taken place in that very courtyard while inside, behind us, diners laughed, and silverware clinked against dishes.

Marie lit a cigarette and brushed a strand of sweat-soaked hair from her eyes. Even like this, in a grease-stained uniform with her hair tied up in a knot on top of her head, she was a pretty girl. She was also mentally bright, a talented cook, a hard worker,

189

and had a good future ahead of her—if you didn't factor in her scheduled demise. Well, that was no longer a consideration. I had decided otherwise. All on my own. I hadn't told the others in my clan. They believed that she would die this very night. That in a few moments I would take the blood that I needed, draining her beautiful form, ending its animated state, leaving her a pale, limp corpse.

Well, that wasn't going to happen. I had grown weary of my eternal existence. I yearned for the finality of death. Call it romanticism, if you will. I aspired to be like the poets, who rage for a day and then perish into endless night. I literally craved the delirium of oblivion.

My mind was made up. She would not die prematurely that night. And I would live out my remaining days, however few, in the luxury of knowing that they were finite, limited by nature.

Marie took a drag off her cigarette, then tossed back her head and exhaled a stream of smoke into the cloudless sky. I saw Saturn winking brightly through the rising haze. I hoped she quit soon. Smoking was bad for her.

Her break was over. She returned to the hot kitchen, not realizing she had been granted a pardon from the inexorable machinery of doom. I savored my last swallow of wine, returned the empty glass to my table, paid my bill and walked out to my parked car. The heat hadn't eased up any with the coming of sundown. I would soon be stretched out on my bed—sans sheets—my eyes shut, sweating, on the edge of dream, imagining the life that lay ahead for Marie.

THE FLOWER MAIDENS

Bee swarms effervesce,
in clouds coalesce,
in gardens of abandoned desire,
while pulpy blossoms conspire
gratification's delay
in a languid display
of burgeoning tumescent desire,
in their most damning floral attire.

Inquire of the flowers,
their hypnotic powers,
when the moon is at its height,
in the luminous pollen-rich night,
and they'll whisper a song
of the saffron-headed throng
rippling in the blazing star light,
waving in the numinous night.

The shapely flower lasses
who sprout from the grasses
while the hills are drenched in moon glow,
as the saps of the succulents flow,
exude fragrance alluring
to those not demurring,
enticing with narcotic delights
as verdant floral passion ignites.

APPARITION FROM THE
BONEYARD

Providence, 1848

On a sultry summer evening, feeling unsettled and confined in his hotel room, Edgar Allen Poe takes to the streets in search of cooler air and spiritual serenity. Wandering up College Hill along Benefit Street, he descends a cobblestone lane and enters the small, secluded eighteenth-century churchyard that lies behind the Cathedral of Saint John. He believes himself to be alone—unless one counts as company the resident shades of the two hundred departed souls who lie therein interred. In some unfathomable manner the slanting and fallen headstones with their curious antique designs and somber, lichen-encrusted inscriptions provide a temporary solace to his deeply troubled heart. At the rear of the yard near a stone embankment that boarders the edge of the burial ground, a gnarled willow grips its claw-like roots into the hallowed earth. Halfway up the hill to Benefit Street and behind the tree is a wooden bench on a raised path providing a view of the churchyard below as well as the Cathedral, which at this hour is unoccupied and gloomy with shadows. Up until this moment, Edgar had not noticed the solitary woman sitting on the bench, gazing at him intently as

193

he rambles the aisles, silently reading the sorrowful words on the markers. There is something familiar and yet extraordinary about this pale feminine apparition; she might be a beautiful distant cousin of his, or a pallid angel of mercy—he is uncertain. Her form is slender and slight, her silky tresses the color of sand when the tide has receded. And, he notes with perverse satisfaction, her ashen skin is radiant—almost glowing—but sallow, as if she is caught in the grip of an unspeakable terminal affliction, and the fires burn bright within the caldron of her soul. He resolves that her uncanny appearance augers well, foretelling the imminence of that which he seeks more than anything else in this world. Alive with frenzied anticipation, he scrambles past row after row of disordered headstones and races up the rough-hewn rock staircase at the back of the church so as to engage this enigmatic sprite, but when he stumbles into the elevated courtyard adjoining the raised path, he sees that the bench that she had so recently occupied is now abandoned, and his ashy seraph is gone.

From his vantage place in the shadowy courtyard, Edgar can see into a small moonlit rose garden occupying a plot behind the last house on Benefit Street before it meets with Church Street. He momentarily considers entering the garden, imagining the rich fragrance of its blossoms under the blazing stars, but he understands it to be a private plot, so instead he exits the courtyard and positions himself for a while on the sloping brick sidewalk along Church Street, staring up at the red corner house as if expecting someone to appear on its side porch. And appear, she does: Sarah Helen Whitman, the dark-haired, widowed poetess, draped in flowing silks and diaphanous scarves, black satin slippers on her feet, her face strangely veiled in the manner of one who divines the future and communicates with the spirits of the dead. After a moment she lifts the mystic veil from her lovely face and sighs deeply, tilting her head far back to breathe in the serene night air, then raises a dainty handkerchief to her flared nostrils and sharply inhales the sweet odor of liquid ether in which the cloth has been soaked so as to inspire dreams on a sweltering evening such as this. Well aware of her name and somewhat sensational reputation but not having previously met her—for she was recently pointed out to him by a friend who offered to introduce them—Edgar is suddenly desperately in love with this exquisite creature. He must win her affection, possess her adoration, capture her heart! She observes him standing there, her dusky eyes narrowing with calculation, but says nothing until eventually he turns away and walks off, already mentally composing a letter he imagines he will write to her, proposing a daytime meeting in the churchyard. Its opening lines are upon his lips, his eyes wide in metaphysical wonder and sensual desire as he ecstatically staggers away into the night. Meanwhile, Sarah Helen has left the porch and returned to the intimacy of her parlor where, after she has concluded the séance she has been conducting for a cadre of close women friends and is finally alone at midnight, she will compose ardent verses memorializing her mysterious new suitor, the quixotic Edgar.

Unobserved by any living being, the fey angel of mercy that Edgar had lately glimpsed from below, the macabre cherub who had vanished upon his excited pursuit and in the process had knowingly and with preternatural cunning led him to gaze upon the visage of the winsome and seductive Sarah Helen as she took the night air on her porch, now emerges from her imposing russet sepulcher in the heart of St. John's Churchyard and slowly ascends the stone steps into the lonely courtyard, then silently goes down another flight of stairs and traipses onto the brick walkway of Church Street, where she will follow Edgar from a distance, a supernatural usher of whom he is only subliminally aware. Were there any persons loitering about who might witness her weird passage, they would shriek in horror at the sight thus presented, for she is arrayed in the tattered ruins of her burial shroud, and

195

her face, which Edgar believed to be sweetly fetching, they would perceive truly as lost to corruption and the ravages of the worm, for her flesh is beyond rotted and in a pathetic state of advanced decay, its whitish tint that he had found so tenderly attractive actually being the vile shade of yellow that one sees in the parched skins of ancient corpses, if one is in the questionable habit of extended lingering within forsaken necropoli.

THE SUMMONS

On wind-swept nights
do spirits linger,
extending forth
a decayed finger?

To prod the living
from their slumber,
a call to join
their spectral number?

Teeming at the
ancient gates,
to burst the bolts
where Death awaits?

Emissaries from
the ebon tomb,
dragging souls
to eternal doom?

This I ask on
gust-chilled eves,
when something stirs
midst rotted leaves.

The Hag's Revenge

Boston, 1827

Cadet Edgar Allen Poe had been drinking for five hours when the fight broke out. He was down to his last few coins and made the terrible mistake of asking a burly man at the neighboring table if he was interested in hearing a true story about a haunted warehouse in the neighborhood, which Poe would be happy to tell for the price of a glass of cognac. The fellow took unreasonable offense at this friendly offer and expressed his displeasure by pummeling Poe with the heavily callused fists that come from years of manual labor on the docks. Poe soon found himself sprawled on the filthy floor with a bleeding lip and a loose tooth. Adding insult to injury, the proprietor of the seedy establishment in which he had been progressively sinking deeper and deeper into a melancholy depression viewed the altercation as entirely Poe's fault, and promptly threw him into the rat-infested alley in which the nameless public house occupied a particularly unsavory space between two larger, decaying buildings that dated back to the eighteenth century, if not colonial times.

Dusting himself off before gingerly touching his swollen mouth to determine the extent of his wounds, Poe staggered along the dark and narrow alleyway for a considerable distance, hoping that another tavern with a more amiable clientele would soon present itself. He found nothing of the sort, only an endless succession of empty, derelict structures that appeared to be on the brink of collapse as they leaned precariously against one another. The alley eventually came to a dead end, at which point a second, narrower, and darker alley branched off from it, headed in the direction of Boston Harbor, if he was not mistaken. He knew he was in the North End, somewhere north of Prince Street, but exactly where, he wasn't sure. The entire district was a confusing and disorienting maze of interconnecting alleys at the street level, with an extensive network of dank cellars, primitive tunnels, ancient burial crypts, and other less reputable subterranean spaces underlying it.

Over the months since he had arrived in Boston, Poe had heard whispered legends claiming that subhuman canine-like ghouls that walked on their hind legs occupied the more remote portions of this underground metropolis—strange, demonic, corpse-eating beasts who regularly communed with the nearby Copps Hill Burial Ground. He didn't give such eerie tales much credence, although he supposed that such an abomination was scientifically possible, given the wide variety of extreme biological adaptations already known to modern science. This second alley which he had been following ultimately branched off to a third and then fourth alley, their courses twisting and turning in such an unpredictable manner that Poe began to fear that he was losing his bearings, but then, thankfully, the last of these seemingly endless alleys spilled out onto the main thoroughfare of historic Hull Street, and soon he found himself climbing the stairs up to one of his favorite local haunts, the centuried cemetery at Copps Hill.

The full moon, appearing larger than usual at that early morning hour, shone with such a bold, silvery light that Poe could read almost all the inscriptions carved on the ancient grave markers, excepting those that were heavily weathered and worn almost smooth by the centuries of rain, sleet, and snow that had fallen on their silent faces. He wove his way up and down the familiar rows of headstones, stopping now and then to enjoy a fondly remembered inscription or an especially charming carving depicting an angel, skull, dancing skeleton, weeping willow, or some other reminder of the fragility and transitory nature of human life. In due time he spotted ahead the outline of the most notable tomb in the burial ground: the final resting place of three members of the notorious Mather family: Increase and his son Cotton—both influential Puritan ministers who played an unfortunate role in the Salem witchcraft trials of 1692—as well as the grandson Samuel. Poe sought out the Mather tomb whenever he visited Copps Hill. Situated near the Charter Street gate on the opposite side of the yard from where he had entered, the Mather crypt was an imposing aboveground container of red brick topped with brown stone and enclosed within a wrought-iron fence of modest height. When he was close enough to lean over the fence and examine the tomb, he was at first confused by the disorder he saw there, and then dismayed, for it had been scandalously vandalized since his last visit. Among other damage, one of the two slate squares that contained the Mathers' engraved names had been shattered, and an entire corner comprising one-fourth of the square was missing, so that only the letters "*Co*" remained of Cotton's name.

Who would do such a vile and senseless thing, he wondered? This grievous insult to the memory of these historic persons filled Poe with outrage and offended his refined sensibilities. His first instinct was to look for the absent piece or pieces. Searching the area surrounding the violated tomb, he soon found the missing parts of the slab: it had been smashed into three smaller fragments, apparently by being hammered upon with the broken-off top half of a small, eighteenth-century infant's headstone, which lay discarded nearby.

Poe gathered up these scattered chunks of slate and hastily returned them to their rightful position atop the Mather tomb, temporarily restoring the inscription to read "*The Reverend Doctors Increase, Cotton, & Samuel Mather were interred in this Vault. 'Tis the Tomb of Our Fathers ...*" etc., etc. As he did so, he heard a cacophony of muted feminine voices coming from the closest perimeter of the graveyard. Glancing over toward Charter Street, he was startled to see what appeared to be a veritable troupe of modern-day witches, no doubt entering the yard with the intent of performing some new illegitimate mischief of an unpredictable nature.

Not wishing to engage these nocturnal interlopers in conversation, Poe receded into a pitch-black area not far from the Mather tomb and slumped down roughly against an old gravestone, from which vantage point he hoped to watch these women without being observed himself. His lips felt terribly dry and parched, and from his belly came the persistent craving for a fresh sip of some agreeable beverage. Happily, he suddenly remembered the ornate silver flask that he habitually carried in an inner pocket of his frock. Hopefully, it still held an adequate amount of whiskey. Retrieving the flask, Poe unscrewed its cap, raised the container to his lips, and was pleased by the pleasurable sensation of a generous mouthful of fiery liquid flowing across his tongue and down his thirst-tormented throat.

The witches slowly progressed along an unpaved path toward the Mather tomb. Something about the odd way they moved seemed highly uncanny to Poe. Their unsettling posture, the disturbing movements of their limbs, did not resemble that of wholesome, respectable women. Rather, they ambulated awkwardly and with excessive deliberateness, much the way a wounded wild creature of the woods might shamble, their stiffened limbs shifting suddenly this way and that, their bent frames lurching forward and then hesitating a bit too long before shifting again. And their voices did not possess the natural womanly warmth that one so enjoys when a beloved sister or a comely young wife speaks words of comfort and devotion. Instead, he was listening to the ugly, rasping croaks of a pack of appallingly aged, vagrant crones.

At the forefront of this suspect group, leading the way, was a short, stout hag with frizzled gray hair that stuck profusely out of the cowl of her cape. Her shrill voice rose high above the others, inciting them in the harshest of terms to take their merciless revenge upon not only the Mather tomb, but also the very souls of the long-deceased Mather clan.

"Especially that vile Puritan hypocrite, Cotton, who believed not in the validity of the spectral evidence claimed by a lot of silly, vindictive maidens, but stood aside, mute, and spoke not against it publicly, allowing our poor, cruelly accused sisters to be condemned to suffer, agonizing long in foul jails and then being indecorously hanged! We shall raise Cotton Mather up from the dust and give him a strong taste of his own bitter medicine, I say!"

"Aye, make him pay for his many crimes against the women of Salem Village!" shrieked a scrawny blonde witch behind her.

"Yar! And also, against the ladies of Ipswich, Gloucester, and Andover!" croaked another hag from the back of the group.

"As well as we free women of old Boston!" cried another.

"There it be, gals! Mather's tomb!"

The crones gathered closely around the vault, leaning in to survey the damage they had done in their last outing to Copps Hill, while they described with delirious anticipation the further harm they now meant to wreck upon the reviled monument.

"But what's this? *What's this here?*" screamed their obese leader, running her fat hands over the top of the tomb and tracing with her fingers the hateful names of the three Mathers buried below. "Some do-gooder hath returned the pieces of broken slate to their former configuration, so that the foul slab again spells out

203

the name of him we particularly loath: Cotton! With one mighty sweep of her powerful arm she brushed the stone fragments off the top of the tomb, sending them flying in all directions.

"The nerve of him who hath done this obscene thing!" groused the blond hag.

"Well, ladies, this shall not stand! Indeed, we've come back to finish the job!" bellowed the head witch.

At that, one of the women who had not yet spoken leaped up on the tomb and squatted down while daintily lifting her black skirt, her bony knees half bent.

She's not going to … thought Poe as he took another pull from the flask. But she did exactly what he feared she might, urinating prodigiously on top of the Mather tomb.

Three other crones followed suit in copycat fashion, shamefully desecrating the tomb. Then the entire mob burst into action, spitting on the tomb, slinging handfuls of mud and clods of soil at it, and bashing stray fragments of crumbling headstones upon its face, with the aim of further obliterating the inscription written there. A chorus of insults accompanied the melee.

"Damn the despicable Mathers to Hell!"

"Flaming Perdition's too good for them! May they eternally kiss the Devil's arse!"

"And all their pious prayers fall upon deaf ears!"

"A curse upon their lying mouths!"

"Double-dealing bastards!"

"Persecutors! Torturers!"

"Oppressors!"

The portly head enchantress allowed this noisy barrage of brickbats and verbal insults to continue for a good two minutes before she finally called the group to order. "Enough, my sisters! Enough! Stop, yer pissing, ye wanton hussies! Our great mistress above requires a certain degree of decorum from us when we beseech her to bestow upon us her magical favors. Cover yer limbs, hold yer water, and shut yer mouths. Lay down yer stones and gobs of filth, for we are about to call forward the specter of Cotton Mather, that he may answer for his offenses!"

A profound hush immediately fell over the assembly.

"Ah, that's more like it," said the fat witch. "Now we may call him to account, goddess willing."

Far above their heads, the fleecy white clouds that had been passing before the moon now parted, allowing the brilliant white lunar orb to shine at its brightest. Poe's immediate thought was that he might be more visible now that the full moon in all its radiance was no longer being intermittently blocked by clouds. He hastily scooted around behind the headstone which he had been slouched against, hoping it would fully conceal him from the witches' view.

Still unaware of Poe's presence, the lead sorceress tilted her head far back and stared up lovingly at the glowing moon. She spread out her arms as if to embrace the entire sky, then began to chant in a low, solemn timbre that at first was so guttural that Poe could not make out any of her words, but after a while its pitch rose and its volume increased, so that gradually he began to understand the words she was intoning, although the expressions she used were so odd that he did not gain much sense from them. Whatever she was saying, it seemed to be a prayer or an invocation that was spoken directly to the moon above, asking the goddess whose material form it represented to descend to this graveyard and assist the witches in raising the spirits of the two elder Mathers: Increase and Cotton. Apparently, the witches had no argument with the Mather grandson, and were content to allow him to rest in peace.

At the dramatic height of the head witch's hypnotic incantation, the entire body of witches fell into a pattern of call and response, with the fat witch speaking a phrase that was like the lyric of a song and her followers replying in kind, then another

205

phrase, and another reply, until as a whole they were reciting a charged rhythmical ritual that made Poe's skin crawl. What was he witnessing there? Was some forbidden form of Black Magic being performed before his very eyes? He thought such perverse arcane practices had ceased a century and a half ago, if not in the Middle Ages. At the very height of their incantatory ceremony, a thunderous, ear-piercing boom filled the air, and the Mather tomb was showered in a beam of cold, silvery light that poured down out of the sky from the distant lunar disk, which had swollen to three times its normal size. The witches all fell to their knees, weeping in joy, uttering prayers of gratitude and unconditional love for their great mistress. Even the obese witch sank awkwardly to her knees—her arms still lifted to the heavens—while shouting cries of praise and thanks.

Then something truly miraculous happened. Or he was dreaming all this nonsense in a drunken stupor? Poe wasn't sure which it was, but from the defaced stone surface of the ancient Mather tomb, a misty cloud of light-infused vapor billowed up into the chilly night air. It gradually took the form of a male ghost attired in the garb of a seventeenth-century Puritan ecclesiastic. Black robes, long white collar, wide brimmed hat. This was none other than the shade of the long-deceased Cotton Mather.

Behind Cotton another figure, much fainter, soon formed: the apparition of his father, Increase Mather, also shrouded in ministerial attire. This second ghost flickered in and out of visibility, finally fading into nothingness. But Cotton's phantom persisted.

Silence fell over the witches. Their eyes grew wide in near disbelief. One or two gasped softly.

"Aye, that's the bugger," uttered the crone who had first urinated on the tomb.

"There ye be all high and mighty, Mister Cotton Mather," said the head witch. "Finally called to answer our charges."

The ghost of Cotton began to speak falteringly in his own defense, saying "All my acts ... were done for the glory of God ... and to save Salem Town ... from the predations of Satan..." but before he could finish, the head hag cut him off, addressing her circle of witches more than him.

"We need no further testimony concerning misdeeds and sins of omission committed by Cotton Mather, for the record is abundantly clear. We find you guilty of many crimes, foul sir, many crimes indeed! Falsely arresting the fair ladies of Salem and other towns hereabouts. Torturing false confessions from them with yer brazen lies and application of harsh instruments of pain. Fraudulently convicting them of felonies for which they bore no guilt. Maliciously sentencing them to the most terrible deaths, and smugly watching without mercy as they were hung in the abhorrent manner of murderers."

"Guilty! He's guilty!" screamed one of the witches.

"Aye! Guilty!"

"Hang him!"

"Bring forth the noose!"

"Make him choke on his own tongue as his eyeballs pop from their sockets!"

As they shouted their invective and called for his immediate punishment, each of the hags began to direct toward the late witch hunter the powerful might of their intense hatred and outrage. The combined force of their collective resentment hit Cotton's ghost like a succession of electrical bolts, crackling and popping, causing him to violently twist and turn and writhe in agony. Piercing cries of anguish escaped his throat, while his limbs twitched spasmodically. Poe wondered what the end result of this mass psychic assault would be. The Puritan icon was already dead; could he be further annihilated?

Thoroughly enjoying this well-deserved attack on an abusive figure of authority, the witches jeered and shrieked as they continued their group molestation of Cotton. But neither they nor Poe would learn what the ultimate effect of such an action would be, for at that moment a patrolman of the Boston Watch, strolling along Charter Street at the edge of the burial ground, spotted the mob clustered around the Mather tomb and shined his lantern in their direction while calling out, "Hey there, you ruffians! What tomfoolery are you up to?"

Like a pack of plague rats, the unruly witches scattered in all directions, disappearing into the darkness of the surrounding streets and alleys. In a matter of seconds, the uncanny shade of Cotton Mather silently faded away, leaving the Mather tomb once again in peace and quiet.

Satisfied, the watchman resumed his stroll along Charter Street, and Poe found himself once again alone in the ancient graveyard, surrounded only by the crumbling memorials of The Dead. Bringing out his trusty flask, he took a deep swallow of its precious contents, and then another, before nodding off to sleep.

He was rudely awakened at dawn by the first rays of the rising sun, his body stiff and sore from the beating he had taken, and his head pounding from the worst hangover he had ever had.

A moment later, Poe recalled the fantastical dream he had experience the night before after passing out drunkenly in the secluded spot where he was presently sprawled. It had something to do with the revived spirit of the Puritan minister, Cotton Mather, whose grave lay not fifty feet away. In the dream, Mather was being attacked by an angry horde of modern-day witches. What a farce!

Wait a minute, he mused. *Could this ridiculous hallucination have been real? No, impossible! There are no more witches in Boston. They went out of fashion long, long ago.*

He began to laugh at his own foolishness for having momentarily believed that witches might still exist, but soon discovered that his laughter hurt too much, and so he abruptly stopped. Groaning as he straightened up and slowly rose from the cold earth, Poe began the miserable, hour-long trek back to the Army barracks at Castle Island where he had been stationed since his move to Boston. He was grateful for the small blessing that he was walking away from, rather than into, the painfully rays of the morning sun.

PART 6

HAWAIIAN HORRORS

The Last God

For two centuries, the stone icon lay buried at the bottom of a pit on ceremonial lands where it had been discarded when the people—believing themselves modern—turned against their gods, the idols they had once revered, and overthrew them, toppling their stern effigies, blaspheming their sacred, unutterable names, and insulting their noble memories with vile declarations and despicable indecencies. There, in the silence of the soil, the icon long lay, brooding until the day when Tabor, a humble peasant farmer, was digging a trench to irrigate his crops and struck the stone icon with the blade of his shovel, defacing the carven god with a score across its once-venerated visage.

His discovery of the abandoned lithic deity was long prophesied, having been predicted by those temple priests who, in secrecy, continued to worship in the traditional manner after the old gods had been deposed—smashed and cast asunder— and thus word of what Tabor had found spread like wildfire throughout the land, attracting many seekers who journeyed from afar, coming to the farm to help Tabor in the task of raising the great stone image from the pit wherein it lay. Lifting the weighty stone from the mud of the newly exposed trench with pulleys and ropes and levers, the assembled throng then set it upright, so they might witness the power which it still possessed, and feel the energy it yet exuded, despite the passage of two hundred years

213

underground, out of the sight of men and women, and forgotten by all.

Standing vertically, in a position worthy of a respected god, the icon scowled at the crowd which had gathered around it—the horde of new believers who bowed down in supplication before its crudely chiseled features, paying it homage during the long, hot days, praying to it throughout the cold, star-studded nights. All who looked upon the idol's rough, fearsome face, or turned away in terror from its hateful stare, immediately fell prostrate upon the trembling ground, unable to bear the idol's fierce gaze, convinced of their own unworthiness in its holy presence.

Thus it ruled over the kingdom wherein Tabor dwelled for several ensuing decades, a god incarnate, embodied in a coarsely worked block of volcanic stone fashioned by unknown primitives, resolute in its divinity, beyond questioning, of unchallengeable authority, until one moonless and accursed night when there approached the farm of Tabor a mob of disrespectful profligates who had swept across the land, carrying torches with which they had set ablaze the huts of countless farmers. Coming upon the ancient statue surrounded by a circle of kneeling followers, these rioters attacked, forcing the faithful to flee, then set upon the idol itself, bombarding it with rocks, spitting upon its sanctified countenance, their heretical tongues lashing the god with the vilest of oaths, mocking it, reviling it, before the ultimate indignity of pushing it over, toppling its weighty form and sending it crashing back down into the gloomy pit from whence it had been excavated so long ago.

With screams and yowls the vandals pushed the high piles of dirt surrounding the trench back into the hole, covering the disgraced icon with mounds of earth until the stone was once again buried, as it had been when Tabor first found it that memorable day. Arising with the sun's first rays, Tabor sensed that a terrible evil had befallen his land. Running from his hut, he saw

214

what they had done—the carven stone idol gone, the trench once more filled with dirt and rock—and he fell to his knees in grief, weeping at his misfortune, and the greater loss to his people, now that the last god was dead, slain by the least worthy among them.

WINDS FROM SOME REGION BEYOND

My cousin Ulalee had been living with me for three weeks before she began to disturb me. Make no mistake: I loved her, and most of the time I very much enjoyed her company, but sometimes little things she did irritated me. Like leaving a mess in the kitchen when she fixed herself a meal. Or not rewinding my VHS tapes after watching them in her room with the volume turned up high. Well, actually, in what used to be my bedroom until she moved in with me. I was not about to allow her to become homeless when she phoned me that night, sobbing hysterically that her rent had been doubled, and that she couldn't afford the new amount and had to be out of her place at the end of the month. "There's nowhere for me to go!" she cried. "How am I going to survive on the streets? You know I'm not in good health. I need a roof over my head!"

"Hold on a minute," I said in as reassuring a voice as I could muster. "Take a deep breath. There's no reason for you to be homeless. Not while I have this apartment. You're welcome to stay with me for as long as you like. I have plenty of room."

"You only have the one bedroom. Your place is really tiny."

"Well, yes, it is, but the sofa bed in the living room suits me fine. It's quite comfortable. I've slept on it many times. You'll move in here. I insist. I don't want you to worry about rent or anything else."

And so, she did just that. The next day after work I helped her move her few things out of her old apartment and into my place. This was a much better arrangement for her, financially. She never really could afford her apartment, as cheap as it had been. I had plenty of income compared to her: my pension, my higher Social Security, plus the salary from my part time job at the museum. All she had to live on was her puny Social Security check. No pension at all besides that. And she really couldn't work any longer, not with her health problems. I had enough coming in every month to pay my rent and to feed the both of us, with a little left over, even. She was thrilled by my invitation. It meant she'd have no more money worries. I think she also liked having someone around to talk to if she was in the mood. She had been pretty lonely all by herself in that apartment.

Our day-to-day cohabitation was generally harmonious. She spent most of the time in her room, only coming out occasionally for meals, to do laundry, or for the rare chat, and I kept to the living room. We shared the kitchen and bathroom, although we did not share cleaning duties. That chore fell to me alone.

I really didn't need the bedroom. Everything important to me was out in the living room. A computer on a desk. A TV attached to a VCR. A bookcase holding my personal library. Most nights I read after dinner until I fell asleep. When I wasn't in the mood for reading, I would watch an old movie. I had a couple hundred favorites on tape. I didn't need anything else; that was enough.

*

My apartment was situated on a Waikiki side street, on the practically abandoned grounds of a 1950s Polynesian-themed restaurant and hotel that had fallen on hard times. The restaurant had closed the year before I moved in, but the hotel was still in operation, if somewhat marginally. The hotel no longer had a sign up, and its anonymity along with the rundown condition of the units ensured that it would continue to remain largely vacant for the foreseeable future. I liked the low rent and the location: near the beach, a short drive to the museum, and a corner market down the block. Most of all, I was intrigued by the unusual ambiance of the surroundings. Several large tiki statues were positioned around the property, none of which could be seen from the street, being hidden by overgrown trees, shrubs, and ferns. These towering icons only came into view when I reached the rusty gate of the wrought-iron fence, where I invariably fumbled with my keys for longer than should have been necessary before unlocking the gate and entering.

I worked weekday mornings until noon, ran errands after work, and spent my afternoons at home, usually reading. Most days I sat with a book in a patch of sunlight on the sofa, facing the apartment's front windows. From this vantage point I could look up now and then at the view outside where one of the larger of the courtyard tikis stood on the edge of the grass, off to my left. It was quite solid—monumental, in fact—being about fifteen feet tall. The figure's surface was scalloped in a stylized way that suggested it was a wood carving, but actually, it was made of cast concrete, and must have weighed a ton. From the little I knew about traditional Hawaiian culture, I think it was supposed to represent Kanaloa, God of the Sea, a deity that is associated with fear and the oceans. That seemed appropriate, given how close we were to the water.

Lately, I'd been going through a vintage catalog that described the original founding collection at the museum where I worked. I'd been searching for this rare century-old publication for some time and was delighted when I happened across a low-priced copy at a swap meet near Pearl Harbor. Normally I don't spend my personal time on anything related to work, but this research was an exception. I wanted to become more familiar with the wide variety of historical cultural objects that were housed at the museum. As the database administrator, my primary duty was to update the organization's decrepit 1980s legacy database that stored information on the collection in electronic form, and to run reports from that data when requested by staff or the public. I wasn't expected to know all the details about the catalogued objects themselves, but having a basic historical knowledge of the collection's development and background helped me to sort out issues when I encountered errors or ambiguities in the data. Finding this fragile old paperbound publication was a stroke of luck; copies were seldom offered by rare-book dealers, and when they were, the prices were exorbitant. It was already proving to be a help to me in my daily work—beyond which, it made for pleasurable reading.

*

Late one afternoon, I was sitting on the sofa with a cup of tea, reading the old museum guide, when my attention was suddenly drawn to the giant tiki across the courtyard. The sun was low in the sky, lingering just above the rooftops, and the dark, imposing figure of the ancient deity was silhouetted in stark contrast against the rapidly fading brightness of the sky. Something about the quality of the light at that hour entranced me, conveying as it did an intense physical energy that bordered on the supernatural. I wished the icon were capable of speech, for I longed to ask its secret. But stones do not talk—not even those that were shaped by humans who perished countless years ago and are no longer around to explain them. I had learned that from studying the antiquities housed in the museum. And, I had more recently learned, the same was true of modern reproductions of the ancient statues, such as the hotel's tikis. Although they were originally made to serve as transitory commercial decor, with no intention on the part of their makers that they should play any role in the spiritual lives of the people who daily encountered them, with the passage of time these ersatz icons had begun to take on a life of their own, and they held close to their breast mysterious secrets of their own.

"That thing has you hypnotized," said Ulalee, the cynicism in her tone so routine that it no longer affected me. I hadn't noticed that she had come out of the bedroom a moment before and was now standing behind me.

"That it does. The first few months I lived here, I ignored it, but over time it's grown on me. It's not a very authentic copy of a traditional Tiki statue, and it shouldn't have any *gravitas*, any power, and yet it does. I stare at it and wonder what it's thinking, what it feels."

"I'll tell you what it's thinking: 'I wish these seagulls would stop making a mess on my head.'"

"No, that doesn't bother it. It's tolerant of the seagulls. After all, it's the god of the oceans; seagulls come with the territory. Something else is on its mind. Maybe it's planning our demise."

"It damn well better not be. I'll go out there with a sledgehammer and bust off its nose."

"I would advise against that. Respect must be shown. You don't want to aggravate the gods."

"Whatever. Are we out of ketchup? I'm having that frozen fish for dinner, but only if there's ketchup."

"I think I used the last of it yesterday."

"Okay. I'll have a chicken pot pie instead."

She went into the kitchen, and I heard the sound of the freezer door being opened. By then, the delicate mood of the moment was ruined. I lowered my eyes and went back to reading.

*

221

Normally I brought a sack lunch to work and ate at my desk, but that day I decided to splurge and have a burger in the museum café. The weather was already hot, and the humidity was high due to the trade winds having fallen off over the past few days. I was grateful for the two large pedestal fans that were running in the café. They were unusually noisy, constantly rumbling like a strong wind blowing on a high cliff, but they did cool the place down. In a few minutes my burger was ready, and I carried it over to a corner table away from the other customers, who were a mix of tourists and museum staff with whom I didn't socialize. As a retiree, working in a temporary position, the other employees did not consider me to be their equal and thus worth hanging out with. Beyond which, I was in the Information Technology department, which further qualified me for shunning by most of the museum staff. I was used to this isolation—it made little difference to me. It spared me the bother of having to make small talk with people I barely knew. I was content to sit alone, minding my own business.

Although I was reluctant to leave the comfort of the fans, my break was only a half hour long, so when I finished the burger, I headed back toward my office in a nondescript building behind the impressive museum structure, but first I took a detour through the main exhibit hall. There was a placard for one of the historic objects located in a side gallery that I wanted to read to see if it would shed any light on a cryptic description for the item in the database.

The object in question was a crudely carved basalt icon of the Hawaiian god of wind, Paka'a. It was in an isle between two lit glass cases that were filled with smaller icons and ritualistic objects. The figure stood about four feet tall—not nearly as large as the rare towering antique wooden icons that stood at the end of the main hall, but still imposing, both in its stature and the fierceness of its expression. The few times I had seen this idol,

I had experienced an intense emotional reaction to it: a strange combination of raw, visceral terror and morbid fascination. As a physical object, the statue projected a strong sensation that I can only describe as appalling malevolence—a raging fury—as if it were alive and bore a fervent animosity toward anyone who dared to enter its presence. What puzzled me was the glaring discrepancy between its description in the database, which was short, matter-of-fact, and entirely mundane, and the longer, more detailed, and highly suggestive description for the same object that I had read the night before in the old museum catalog. I wanted to see which way the placard wording leaned. It turned out to be somewhere between the sparseness of the database description and the romanticism of the catalog entry, hinting at some lingering mystery shrouding the object's history, but providing few factual details. I wrote down the text as it appeared on the placard in the pocket notebook I always carried and then left the stately museum edifice and returned to my small office in the humdrum "Library & Archives" building out back.

*

That evening as I sat on the sofa, sipping wine from a mug and staring at our garden tiki as it basked among the ferns in the moonlight, Ulalee suddenly emerged from her bedroom, attired only in a sheer nightgown that revealed more of her charms than she may have realized, and stood by the window, her small hand gently touching the bunched folds of the curtain, pensively staring at the enigmatic concrete icon on the lawn. She turned to me, tilted her head to one side, and whispered, "Do you think it actually regards us? That it cares one way or the other what we do or *say?*"

"I don't know. Perhaps. It seems to have a subtle presence of some kind. I can almost feel it out there, but maybe I'm just imagining that. That feeling might not be a real thing. I know

223

I wouldn't show it any disrespect. That would be pushing your luck."

"Yeah, maybe it would be. I was watching a TV show, but became bored, so I started reading one of your old paperback novels, but it was draggy. And then I had the weird idea that I should come out here and look at that damned thing in the garden. Crazy, huh?"

"No, not crazy. I understand."

She was backlit by pale moonlight, the contours of her still alluring figure made obvious by the translucent fabric of the nightgown. A mild breeze flowing through the screen door caused strands of her shoulder-length hair to gently brush against her cheek, wispy brown strands becoming caught at the corner of her mouth. Something about the scene reminded me of a night many years ago when we were both much younger. We had been drinking in a bohemian tavern with a group of artists and poets, and at one point we went out by ourselves onto an isolated beach—just the two of us wandering about on the smooth expanses of sand— and we stayed out there for hours. I don't remember much of that night, but I do know that eventually we became intimate. In retrospect, it was unthinkable: an abomination. We were related, for heaven's sake; cousins, but also lovers—for that one night, at least. Later, we laughed it off and pretended to forget that it had even happened, but ever since, a certain tension has remained between us. One that is not entirely unpleasant; it can be playful even at times. The knowledge that such a thing was always possible, although I was pretty sure it wouldn't happen again. And now, here she was, living with me, in close daily contact. Probably both of us with too much history behind us to ever act that impulsively again, but still—anything might happen if you gave free rein to your imagination. No! I didn't want to think about her in that way! That regrettable act of momentary weakness has caused me much shame and self-loathing over the years, and sometimes I almost despise her for having allowed it to occur, but then I, too, was fully responsible for what had transpired. I didn't want her to know I was thinking back to that night long ago, and so I changed the subject, asking what book she had been reading.

"Oh, one of your trashy occult thrillers, *The Gusting*, by some wordy aristocratic woman—I forget her name."

"The great Esme Van Lorncroft. That's actually one of my favorite novels. Admittedly it starts off rather slowly, and her prose often is too ornate, but about fifty pages in the story becomes really interesting. It's historical fiction, loosely based on true events in the life of a nineteenth-century poet, Triston Osbourne Vesel, who lived not far from here in the Manoa Valley. Vesel shared a primitive grass hut with his half-sister, Dona Terese Vesel, and there are rumors they had an incestuous relationship, although there's no proof of it. What is clear is that he was inordinately fond of her. She accompanied him on all of his travels, including three European tours and two years of sailing the South Seas, with brief stays on several islands. I don't want to spoil the story for you, but it ends tragically."

"Go ahead, spoil it. I don't mind, and maybe you'll convince me to pick it up again."

"Well, for the final decade of his life, Vesel seems to have been impotent, and the constant nearness of his beautiful sister, whom he adored to distraction, apparently drove him mad, because as much as he desired her, he couldn't have her. Ultimately, he pushed her off a cliff, killing her. At his trial, he blamed the wind for his terrible actions. Said that it whispered constantly in his ear, blowing as it does day and night in that valley. That's why the novel's called *The Gusting*: the nonstop wind drove him to commit murder."

"Was he convicted?"

"No. Strangely, there was a witness who swore that Dona accidentally slipped when she came too near to the edge and was not pushed. Although Vesel had confessed to the crime, there was enough doubt in the jury's mind that they found him not guilty. He lived out the last three years of his life in the hut, alone, writing poem after poem about his lost love. Those poems practically drip with self-loathing and guilt, the poor bastard."

"Does that straw hut still exist?"

"Yes, it does, somewhat miraculously. It's behind a closed tearoom that has an interesting history in its own right. I've been there many times. It's one of my favorite places on the island."

"Take me there!" demanded Ulalee. "I promise I'll finish the book."

"It's a deal. We can go tomorrow. I'll pack a picnic lunch. You'll love the place, and the book, too."

*

We parked in the surrounding residential neighborhood and walked up the long driveway, past an empty parking lot, and into the teahouse grounds. We didn't see anyone around, which was understandable, as the teahouse had closed after a bad windstorm had ripped off sections of the roof a few years ago, but two trucks belonging to a construction company were parked in front of the teahouse.

"Are we allowed in here?" asked Ulalee.

"There's no 'Keep Out' sign, so I take that to mean it's open to the public. If anyone asks what we're doing here, play dumb and say we came for lunch."

The teahouse was a quaint, sprawling one-story building from the 1920s. A sign saying "*CLOSED*" was taped on the inside of the glass door at the main entrance. Peeking through the begrimed windows, it was clear the business had shut down in a hurry. The dining rooms were still full of tables and chairs, and the walls were covered with antique paintings along with decades-old black-and-white photographs and other memorabilia in frames. Several of the photos were of Triston and Dona Vesel.

"Looks like a nice place to eat," said Ulalee.

"It had great reviews. I wish I'd known about it while it was still open. The grass hut is around back," I said, nodding toward the stone stairway on our right that led to an elevated area behind the restaurant. That area was lushly vegetated, almost jungle-like, and the wind seemed to hit it harder than the lower portions of the property.

Ulalee raced ahead of me, then ran from window to window, looking inside the small hut.

"Oh, this is wonderful! It's furnished as if they were still living here."

"Yes, the owners did a nice job of restoring it. The hut was pretty much flattened in the last storm, but they rebuilt it accurately down to the last detail and furnished it with Vesel's belongings." I caught up with her, and together we peered through the hut's only door—which was a modern metal and glass one— to the modest furniture in the sparse one-room structure.

"That's his desk on the right, with his oil lamp and inkstand, and to the far right is his table, set with his original dishes and silverware."

My cousin pointed out with glee the bed on the left side of the room. "And that must be where they did the deed, night after night until he couldn't keep it up anymore!"

"No doubt they shared that bed, unless the incest allegations are false, in which case he probably slept on a cot that's no longer extant."

As we talked, a stiff wind roared relentlessly in our ears. It was easy to understand how it might have driven poor Vesel mad after a while. The babbling gale was very much like a voice whose speech was unintelligible, and the listener's mind, at first confused, then desperately frustrated by the nonsense of the squall, began to imagine a stray word in English here and there, then full phrases, and soon complete sentences—all of them demented utterances from some alien region beyond sanity.

"This damned wind would drive anyone nuts in short order," she said, laughing. "No wonder he pushed her off the cliff. Sleeping in the same bed every night, unable to possess her—and she was a raving beauty according to those photos we saw—the winds of Hell speaking wild idiocy at him. Who could blame the guy?"

"There is a lot of sympathy for his unhappy fate among the readers of obscure books of verse," I observed.

We sat on the edge of the porch, our feet dangling among the ferns bordering the hut's foundation, and I handed her a sandwich from the basket I'd carried from the car.

Then I took out the wine bottle, pulled its cork, and handed it to Ulalee.

"Just a few sips to wash down the food. We don't want to become drunk this early in the day."

"Agreed," she said, wiping her mouth with the back of her hand and passing the bottle back to me.

I took a long pull, then jammed the cork back in. "We can finish this later at home."

*

On Sunday, I drove Ulalee to a sacred stone temple site located on a broad, grassy cliff overlooking the North Shore. She had finished the book the night before and wanted to see mores places associated with Triston Vesel and his sister. The site was reached by a narrow paved road leading up from the coastal highway. I parked in a gravel lot at the road's end, and we walked about fifty feet to the edge of the massive stone platform. Hardly anyone was there—only one other couple.

"This is where he first spoke to Dona of death," I told my cousin.

Ulalee gave me a questioning stare.

"He told her that two hundred years ago natives had sacrificed maidens here under the watchful eyes of their carven gods. Slit open their bellies by the light of the bonfires, while the demonic winds howled."

"On these very stones?" asked Ulalee.

"Yes."

"What did she think of that?"

"Naturally, it frightened her, but—curiously—also aroused her, if you can believe what he wrote in his poems."

"They were here at night," said Ulalee in a flat, matter-of-fact tone, gazing around as she imagined the scene.

"Yes, midnight. The place was abandoned. Dona stripped down and ran naked among the hundreds of stones until she found one that was larger than the rest and somewhat elevated. Unexpectedly, she lay upon it lengthwise, flat on her back, and called out to Triston, 'Is this where they did the killing?' To which he silently nodded *Yes!*"

"She must have been half insane," suggested Ulalee.

"I think so."

Although it was forbidden, according to signs posted around the site, Ulalee walked a short distance out onto the platform and sat on a stone facing me, her back to the sea below and her legs crossed. She lit a cigarette and slowly exhaled a stream of smoke that the wind quickly pulled away.

"I don't recall a scene like that in the book," she said, her eyes narrowing to slits.

"For some reason it's not in the novel," I replied, "but Vesel talks about it in his poems."

"Do you have his book of poetry?"

"Yes, a first edition."

"I want to borrow it."

"Sure, as long as you promise to handle it carefully. It's very rare. By the way, don't …," I began, intending to warn her not to crush out her cigarette against the sacrifice stone, but she did just that before I could finish the sentence.

"Hm?" she said, raising her eyebrows.

"Nothing."

She rose and walked toward the parking lot, the wind pressing her skirt tight against the back of her legs and making it billow out in front of her. As we neared the car, I could hear a stream of babbling spectral nonsense emerging from the rising gale, something about the cotton of her dress and the smoothness of her thighs, but I did my best to ignore it.

*

Our weekend adventures had me thinking about the museum's mysterious icon of Paka'a, the wind god, and the strange, disturbing feelings it had stimulated in me when I was in its presence. On Monday I used my morning break to walk over to the exhibit hall and take a fresh look at the roughly fashioned stone effigy standing rigidly erect against the wall at the end of a shadowy aisle between two glass cases. I wanted to ask it why the island's winds tormented men, raising dark thoughts of illicit chaos and insatiable desire in their hearts, goading them to frenzies of mayhem and murder, but I dare not speak aloud lest the nearby security guard overhear my utterance and think me deranged.

I psychically asked the icon to grant me understanding, forming the question silently in my mind, but no reply was forthcoming from the basalt deity. All that issued from the cryptic statue was a negative emotional discharge, as if the thing despised me beyond comprehension and would destroy me if I allowed it to gain dominance over my being.

Giving up for the time being, I headed back to my office, stopping briefly at the museum café to buy coffee. The pedestal fans were running full blast, drowning out the voices of my coworkers as they made small talk.

*

The full moon that night looked twice its normal size and shone with a manic yellow luminosity. I was lounging on the sofa, savoring a glass of wine and gazing out at the huge concrete effigy in the garden, entertaining the irrational idea that perhaps it could somehow help me to understand the malignant force that tormented me whenever Ulalee and I visited a windy site on this enigmatic island.

Clad in her nightgown, her long hair brushed out, she emerged from her room and quietly sat beside me, her hands folded neatly in her lap. A second later, she reached over, placed her right hand on top of my hands as they cradled the wine glass, and leaned forward cautiously, as if to interrupt my reverie as courteously as possible.

I smiled in what I hoped was an innocent manner, trying not to read too much into the situation.

"You said you'd loan me your copy of Triston Vesel's poetry book," she said, "I'm curious to see how he portrayed his sister."

"*Half*-sister," I corrected, immediately regretting my pedantry. "Sure, I'd be glad to."

"*Half*-sister," she repeated with a grin, not seeming to mind my unnecessary concern with minor details. "What's it called?"

"*Winds from Some Region Beyond.* Published in 1897 in an edition of only two hundred copies. I was fortunate enough to find one at an antiquarian bookshop a few years ago. It's right over here." I went to the bookcase, which was deep in shadow, being too far from the windows to benefit from the moonlight.

Ulalee reached over and was about to turn on a lamp by the sofa.

"No need for that," I said, running my fingertips along the

spines of a row of books until I came to one particular volume bound in blue buckram. "I know exactly where it is."

She clicked on the lamp anyway.

"Ah, here we go." I pulled the slender book out and brought it to her.

"It looks fragile," she observed, cautiously taking the book from me with both hands and opening it to the title page.

"Yes. The binding is weak, and the hinges are 'tender,' as the bibliophiles would say."

She snickered at the term. "That almost sounds indecent. 'Darling, what tender hinges you have!'"

We both laughed.

"Oh Lord!" she exclaimed with a disapproving frown when she saw the photograph facing the title page. "He *actually* used a picture of her in the book? What nerve!"

"Indeed. The frontispiece is a beautiful image of Dona taken a year before her death."

"She's truly lovely. Doomed women always are. I wish I had her face, not to mention her figure. And I'd kill for that dress!"

"You're every bit as attractive as she was. Maybe more so."

"You're just saying that because I'm your cousin, and you love me."

"Yes, you are and yes, I do, but I'm not just saying it. It's true."

She leaned over and kissed me on the cheek quite chastely; nonetheless, I blushed.

"I'll be very careful with this," she whispered. "Thank you."

Then she rose, the book clutched in both hands, and disappeared into the darkness behind us.

*

Sometime after midnight I was lying on the pulled-out sofa bed, on my side, facing the hallway running between Ulalee's room and the bathroom. I had been dreaming about some vague, disturbing problem, but upon waking immediately forgot the specifics of it. My eyes were open, but I was not paying attention to anything. By coincidence, Ulalee chose that very moment to dart down the hallway. She had shed her nightgown sometime prior to that and was now completely uncovered. The moon, having changed position in the sky since we had talked, clearly illuminated her unclothed form. This startling sight persisted for only a second, but it left a lasting impression on my mind, and when I fell back to sleep, I dreamed of her. We were on a beach, wandering, lost, and I desired her—madly, intensely, impossibly. The dream was at the same time unspeakably sweet and woefully sorrowful.

*

The mountain lookout where Triston Osbourne Vesel pushed Dona Terese Vesel off a high cliff to her horrible death was a popular spot on the windward side of the island. Ulalee had never been there, and I hadn't planned to show it to her, but after she had read Vesel's poems the night before, I was not surprised when the first thing she said at breakfast was, "Take me to where it happened."

"You're sure it wouldn't be too morbid and depressing?"

"Not at all. I would love to see the scene of the crime, to stand on the precipice, the wind howling in our faces, and visualize how it must have gone down, to imagine his conflicted feelings, the struggle within his soul as he alternately yearned for her, then scorned her, then raged against her, then desired her, body and soul. Please, can we go today?"

A lengthy paved walkway led from the parking lot to a broad stone terrace that overlooked the coastline below with its rocky beaches where the surf pounded angrily. From this vantage point we could see a wide expanse of ocean that extended to the horizon, beyond which rose a bluish-gray sky that seemed troubled by its many clouds. Impatient as an excited child, Ulalee ran ahead of me, the fiercely gusting wind buffeting against her skirt as she raced to the low-walled edge of the platform and leaned out as far as she could with her hair whipping behind her.

"Be careful!" I called out, but I don't think she heard my words over the noise of the wind. When I caught up with her and braced myself against the steel railing, she turned and smiled brightly, shouting "Do I look like her?"

"You mean Dona? Yes, you do."

"I want to *be her,* to balance before the emptiness, my back to the thin air, teetering at the very edge of life, and to feel him—Triston—there, a few feet away, loving me so very much that he is utterly compelled to do something terrible, something unthinkable—whatever it takes to stop the awful gnawing within of his constant, insatiable lust for me!"

"No, Ulalee, you don't really want that. It's a dangerous fantasy, one that should not be played out. You want to live, not to die at the bottom of a cliff on a pile of rocks. That would be tragic, a terrible waste of life. Please don't go any farther."

People on either side were watching us with alarm and yet keeping their distance.

"Closer!" she yelled, struggling to be heard over the roaring wind. "I want to be closer!"

At the end of the wall was a narrow gap between it and the edge of the mountain, an opening just large enough for a person to squeeze through. Without hesitation, Ulalee ran to the gap and wiggled through, then scrambled down a narrow dirt trail that looped back to a lower ledge located ten feet below the main terrace. I had no choice but to follow, lest she foolishly encroach too far and accidentally slip off that railless ledge.

The wind was even wilder there, and I doubt she heard anything I said as I carefully tottered toward her, pleading all the while for her to step away from the cliff.

234

"Damn it, Ulalee! You're going to end up dead! Please come away from the edge. Don't go any farther!"

But she was determined, standing less than a yard from where the rock began to abruptly curve downward, her back to the void, arms held out like a circus performer on a high wire, her eyes closed. She suddenly took another step backward, bringing her to a point only a foot from where the rock's surface began to slope downward, and I gasped.

With far greater caution than she had just shown, I slowly inched toward her, repeatedly begging her to step forward toward me, away from the perilous brink. I was terrified she might lose her footing and fall backward, might plunge a thousand feet down onto the rocks, but somehow, she didn't.

Throughout it all, the wind buffeted madly against us, pushing our frail bodies toward their inevitable destruction, and buried within its constant erratic babbling were the chaotic strains of a chorus of cold, inhuman voices that urged me to extend my hand toward Ulalee but an inch or two, to touch her gently, almost lovingly, with barely any force, just enough to upset her balance by the smallest degree, so that she might fall.

Did I alone hear them, this depraved multitude declaiming in unison, this assembly of mad angels uttering blasphemous demands so difficult to resist that in frantic denial I finally clasped my hands over my ears, and yet still I heard them incanting?

O, they intoned, *it is a loving act!*

Do not fear! they implored. *She whom you adore yearns for your touch!*

Do not deny her your exalted kindness! they moaned.

And as they chanted, a dreadful vision filled my mind—the stern visage of Paka'a, Hawaii's stony god of wind, decreeing that I obey their bidding.

At that moment, Ulalee opened her eyes extremely wide and beamed maniacally, and I thought—oh God!—that she might

235

allow herself to fall backward, or that I might succumb to the commands of the demons and give her the fatal shove we both knew was looming, but thankfully neither of those unthinkable possibilities materialized.

Instead, my beloved cousin finally stepped forward, wrapped her arms tightly about me, and with a great swelling of emotion I, in turn, hugged her dearly, then led her back to the dirt trail and up to the safety of the stone terrace with its sturdy wall and rigid railing.

We spoke little of this incident on the drive home. All I dared to say was that we would never return there, and she agreed that was wise. However, she did assure me that she very much appreciated seeing where Dona Vesel had been pushed to her death by her half-brother, Triston Osbourne Vesel, on that fateful day over a century ago.

finis

Acknowledgments

The stories and poems in this collection first appeared in the following venues:

The Audient Void: "The Crawling Dead" and "A Visit to the Morelle Family Tomb."

Black Lotus: "Lines Written in the Night Wind."

The Blizzard Rambler: "Upon the Night Ether."

Cyaegha: "Chamber of Shards," "The Crypt of Nitocris," "The Cyprian's Tale," "The Dying King," "The Hour of Transference," "In Her Hibernal Aspect" and "Out of Arkham Hills."

Forbidden Knowledge: Darkness Ascending, ed. Graeme Phillips (Cyaegha Special Publications, 2017): "Innsmouth Bathers."

Nightmare's Realms, ed. S. T. Joshi (Dark Regions Press, 2017): "Beneath the Veil."

Spectral Realms: "Admonishments for the Incautious," "Agents of Dread," "A Billion Souls Gaze West," "Black Panther," "Caressa's Song," "The Flower Maidens," "A Frenzy of Witches," "In Nether Pits," "Innsmouth Shanty," "The Last God," "The Milk Hare," "Oblivion's Daughter," "Painted Ladies," "Procession of the Expendable," "Song for Naughty Children," "The Summons," "Testament of the Scribe," "Those" and "Three Witches."

Weird Fiction Review: "Her Wan Embrace."

"Along that Pallid Path," "Apparition from the Boneyard," "The Hag's Revenge," "Red Wine," "Shroud of Dust and Decay," "Smells of the Nest," "Washed Up," "Winds from Some Region Beyond" and "The Witch Pool" are original to this collection.

About the Author

DAVID BARKER has been writing supernatural fiction and poetry since the mid-1980s. In collaboration with the late W. H. Pugmire, he wrote three books of Lovecraftian fiction: *The Revenant of Rebecca Pascal* (Dark Renaissance Books, 2014), *In the Gulfs of Dream & Other Lovecraftian Tales* (Dark Renaissance Books, 2015) and *Witches in Dreamland* (Hippocampus Press, 2018), all three of which will be published in German language editions by Edition Bärenklau. David's work has appeared in many magazines and anthologies including *Fungi, Cyäegha, Weird Fiction Review, The Audient Void, Nightmare's Realm, Forbidden Knowledge, Spectral Realms,* and *The Art Mephitic.* In 2020 his short story "Who Maketh Fertile the Fields" appeared in *A Walk in a Darker Wood: An Anthology of Folk Horror.* He lives in Oregon with his wife, Judy. They have four daughters.

About the Artist

DAN SAUER is a graphic designer and artist living in Oregon. In 2016, he co-founded (with editor/publisher Obadiah Baird) *The Audient Void: A Journal of Weird Fiction and Dark Fantasy*, which features his design and illustration work. Since 2017, he has worked extensively on book covers and interior art for Hippocampus Press and other publishers. His art often takes the form of surreal collage and photomontage, as pioneered by artists such as Max Ernst, Wilfried Sätty, J. K. Potter and Harry O. Morris. In 2020, he launched his own publishing imprint, Jackanapes Press (**JackanapesPress.com**), which is devoted to publishing odd, antiquarian and eldritch works.

Colophon

The text was set in ADOBE GARAMOND.
Charcuterie was used for titling, ornaments,
and drop caps.

www.ingramcontent.com/pod-product-compliance
Lightning Source LLC
Chambersburg PA
CBHW030406020726
47493CB00003B/960